Crazy About A
COWBOY

Cowboy Hero, Book 4

BARBARA MCMAHON

One

S am Haller saw her across the crowded stockyard in the glare of the noonday sun. Shooting the bull with a bunch of cowhands was part and parcel of the stock sales, and Sam had been leaning against the rail fence, one booted foot resting on the bottom rung, swapping tall tales with the best of them when his gaze was caught.

Dust hung in the air, dry as a desert, churned up by the horses and cattle crisscrossing the stockyard. The background noise of bawling bulls and the occasional shrill whinny of a horse was ignored almost unheard.

In that instant, everything came to a crashing halt. Sam stared, ignoring the other men, the heat of the sun, the cacophony of sound. He felt as if he'd been punched in the gut. Time stood still. Slowly he lowered his foot, standing to his full height, his gaze never moving from her.

Memories flooded his mind; her laugh, her tears, the fights they'd had, the making up, making love long into the night. They'd been crazy in love, crazy in lust or just plain crazy.

It felt as if a vice gripped his heart. He hadn't seen her in two years, except once, briefly, when he'd had to take Joey home early and no ranch hand had been available to deliver him. The jumble of emotions from that day stayed with him for a long time insuring he didn't risk another encounter.

What was she doing in a stockyard in Fort Worth, Texas, when he thought she was in Denver? And who was the man she was talking with? Laughing with.

Jealousy churned as he watched. Was it an illusion? Or the real Lisa? For months after she left, he'd thought he'd spotted her a dozen times. Impossible since she moved away from Texas and on to Colorado. Was this another instance of imagining he saw her everywhere he went?

"Hey, Haller, you going off in a trance?" one of the men in his group asked. The rest laughed, one looking in the direction Sam was staring.

"From the looks of that babe, guess our Sam is finally going to break down and show he's human," another man joked.

Sam scowled and glared at Tim Higgins. He readjusted his Stetson and resumed his casual pose leaning against the fence, though every fiber of his being urged him to take off across the stockyard and confront Lisa. Find out what she was doing in Texas. See her, speak to her. Touch her.

Deliberately he turned away, tried to focus on what the men were talking about. Jeez, he had it bad. Still. They'd been divorced two years. It was over. When was he going to accept it and move on? When was he going to see another woman and really be interested in her?

"If you mean that bay mare, you're right. I wouldn't mind having her. If she throws true, I'd have some fine get," Sam said, hoping to bluff his way through.

One of the cowpokes slapped another on the shoulder. "Should have known Sam's coveting some horse. He never cuts loose like the rest of us."

None of the men present, recent acquaintances, knew about his marriage. He planned to keep it that way. No man liked to admit failure. Especially when it was his own fault.

As soon as he could without causing comment, he offered

to buy everyone a round of drinks at the bar that night and headed off. Deliberately heading away from Lisa, he studied some of the cattle for sale, talked with one man at length about one of the bulls, but his mind wasn't on stock.

It revolved around Lisa. If it had been Lisa, where was she now? Had she left or was she wandering around with that man checking out the sale animals?

A casual glance in the surrounding area let him know he wasn't being observed by anyone. Turning swiftly, he headed for the spot where he'd seen her.

She was gone.

He stood for a moment in indecision, then headed in the direction she'd been facing. In less than ten minutes he caught up with her. She stood to one side, out of the main swirl of traffic, jotting notes in the sales catalog, then glancing up to study one of the bulls penned in the shade.

He hesitated, wanting to speak to her, knowing they had nothing left to say. Hadn't it all been said years ago?

Yet the pull of connection was still there. He tried not to think about her that would drive him crazy. But seeing her again – maybe it was fate.

What could it hurt to just say hi? It wasn't as if they couldn't be civil. Saying hi wasn't a declaration of intent. Not that they had a prayer of getting back together. There was too much between them. More than even Lisa knew.

Almost without volition, his feet carried him in her direction. When he drew close enough to smell her flowery scent over the dusty air and pungent cattle, he halted. It wasn't too late to turn and walk away, she hadn't seen him yet.

But Sam Haller wasn't a coward.

"Hello, Lisa."

She spun around, her eyes widening.

"Sam! I didn't expect to see you."

"What are you doing here, then?"

She tilted her head, her eyes narrowing. "I'm on an assignment for my boss."

"An insurance agent in Denver?" he asked in disbelief.

She shook her head. "I've changed jobs."

He waited, watching as she rolled the catalog up in her hands, unrolled it. Was Lisa as nervous as he felt? He pulled the brim of his hat down a bit lower, tucked his fingers in the back pocket of his jeans, his gaze never leaving her. He tried to ignore the rush of blood through his veins. Damp down the feelings that threatened to rise.

She looked great. Her glossy brown hair held back from her face with clips, fell in waves across her shoulders. The checked shirt was opened at the throat, revealing her pale skin. The snug jeans fit like a second skin. He remembered peeling them off her, touching every inch of her satiny skin as it became revealed.

Swallowing hard, he shifted a bit to ease the growing awareness.

She looked away. "I'm working here in Fort Worth. I missed Texas. And my folks wanted to be able to see Joey more often and more easily."

Joey, their son. A link between the two of them that would never cease.

"As I do, especially now that he's older," Sam said.

She twisted the catalog. "I received the notice from your attorney. Why now? Why change anything? You didn't want him when we separated."

"That's not true. But a baby needs his mother. He's three now and a little boy needs a dad."

"And his mother!" she said, facing him again.

"I never said he didn't. You asked why I was petitioning for more time with him at this juncture. I explained. It'd make it easier if you'd just come back to Tumbleweed."

Easier to deal with Joey, harder to live with the fact their marriage had ended so abruptly. If Lisa was living in town he'd run the risk of seeing her unexpectedly at any time.

"I don't want to do that," she said quickly.

"Why not? It's your home."

It was an argument that had raged for days when she first left. She'd refused to stay in Tumbleweed insisting she needed distance and her own space. So she'd uprooted their baby, said goodbye to all she'd known, and moved to Denver. The distance alone made it almost impossible for a busy rancher to get time to see his son. A subtle way to make her point, but one he'd been powerless to defend against.

"I have a nice apartment here in Fort Worth. And a good job. There's nothing for me in Tumbleweed."

"You had a nice place in Tumbleweed."

"Your ranch?"

"It was ours when we married."

"It was always yours. Yours and Nick's."

At the mention of his brother, Sam's blood began to heat. Nick had been the final straw in their rocky relationship. The brother she should have married, he thought again, remembering their last blowup.

Then remembering all the lonely days and nights since Lisa had left. Once again Sam wondered if she'd hoped Nick would follow her once she was free.

Some perverse gene had him say, "You know, it's probably past time Joey came home to stay. He'll inherit half the ranch, it's time he starts learning about how to run it. It'd be easier if you lived in Tumbleweed. But it doesn't matter. I'm determined to have my son in my home at least half a year. He needs to learn as he grows, not come in cold when he's an adult."

It was something he'd discussed with his attorney. Jason Ronald had advised waiting a bit longer before pushing for joint custody primarily because of the distance between the two households. But all bets were off now that Lisa moved back to Texas.

If he couldn't have his wife, he at least could have his son.

"He's only three. Too young to learn about ranching," she said, almost shaking with sudden anger.

"Joey's as much my son as he is yours. He can learn a lot by observation. Can't start too young," Sam said easily, amazed to hear his voice sound so calm.

He wanted to reach out and snatch her close, hug her against him until she softened and put her arms around him like she used to do. Feel her soft body press against his. Rant and rave at her for leaving. For not wanting him as much as he'd always wanted her.

What would she do if he kissed her until she was pliant and willing and as hot for him as she'd once been.

He was fascinated by the soft curve of her lips, the hint of color high in her cheeks, the flashing blue eyes that glared at him. At least it beat indifference.

But it still hurt.

Where had they gone wrong? Had they ever had enough between them to make their marriage work? Had he been fooling himself for years that what they had was more than a sexual attraction that flared in bed and couldn't sustain itself anywhere else?

"He's too young. He needs-- "

"Lisa! There you are."

Sam turned to look at the man hurrying over to them. It was the same one he'd seen Lisa laughing with earlier. Dark haired, not quite six feet, he looked young maybe twenty-five. Lisa might not think that so young, closer to her age than he was.

His brand new his boots still had the shine on them, despite walking around the dusty stockyard. Sam wasn't impressed. Where had she picked up the urban cowboy?

"I think one of the bulls I wanted is going on the block now," he said eagerly

"Okay, I'm coming." She threw a dark look at Sam. "I'm through here."

The stranger looked at Sam, not picking up on the tension. He smiled and held out his hand. "I'm Bill Taylor. Lisa works for me. You a friend of hers?"

Sam slowly gripped Taylor's hand, his look one of sudden amusement. "You could say that. We go back a long ways. I'm Sam Haller."

Bill looked from one to the other, a puzzled expression in his face.

"Same last name."

"Lisa was my wife," Sam said.

Bill looked from one to the other, then nodded once.

"Lisa just started working for me. She knows a lot about cattle. I unexpectedly inherited a ranch from a distant relative so I really need someone to show me the ropes."

Bill looked from one to another again, obviously at a loss on how to handle the awkward situation.

Sam ignored Bill and glanced at Lisa. "I have work on my ranch," he said. "If you wanted a change from Denver, all you had to do is ask."

"Sorry, I snapped her up first. She's a whiz on the computer and knows more about cattle than I'll probably ever learn," Bill said quickly.

"She staying at your place?" Sam asked.

He didn't like Bill Taylor. And he didn't like knowing Lisa was working for another rancher. What happened to the innocuous office job in Denver? The place that contained more women than men and where the lines of relationships were sharply drawn?

Bill laughed and shook his head, his friendly gaze moving to Lisa.

"No, she won't even consider living on the ranch. She's an independent woman. But I don't need her to ride and rope. The office work can be done anywhere so the set up in her apartment suits me fine. Gives me an excuse to leave the ranch periodically anyway. We better go, Lisa, I don't want to miss that bull."

"I'll be in touch," Sam said, his narrowed gaze on Lisa. "Real soon."

She shook her head but said nothing as she hurried along with Bill Taylor.

Sam watched her hips sway enticingly as she quickly crossed the dirt expanse. Her rich chestnut hair bounced against her back, glossy and shiny in the sunshine. He wanted to tangle his fingers in that silky mass as he used to. He wanted to feel the swell of her hips, the taut, sleek muscles beneath that velvet skin.

He wanted his wife like he'd never wanted anyone--with a hunger that never went away.

Ex-wife.

When was he going to remember that? Or all the complications that made it a certainty that's the way it'd stay?

Sam Haller had been at the sale for two days. He'd be heading home tomorrow with a trailer load of new stock. But now that he knew Lisa lived in Fort Worth, he'd be back.

Lisa hurried to keep up with Bill. He was so enthusiastic about his first auction about every aspect of ranching. Of course he'd only been at it a few months. Wait until he had a hard winter and lost half his herd, or the price of beef dropped to the

8

basement, or anthrax threatened, she thought cynically.

Then frowned. No sense letting Sam get to her. Bill was refreshing to be around, fun, excited, and enthusiastic. She was lucky to get such a great job where she could stay at home or take Joey with her when she needed to visit the ranch. She was doing what she knew and loved.

She'd been miserable in Denver. If she hadn't been so prideful and stubborn, she would never have run so far.

And that's exactly what she'd done, no matter how she tried to dress it up. She'd run like a scared rabbit from Sam and the mess they'd made of their lives.

Dodging a group of cowboys studying a pretty mare, she glanced over her shoulder, wondering if he'd followed them. She couldn't help thinking about Sam. She hadn't expected to see him today. Though if she'd thought about it at all, she knew he went to stock shows all the time constantly on the lookout for good lines to improve his herd. It would have only been a matter of time before she'd run into him at events such at this.

But she'd like to think she'd have been better prepared if she'd had more time. Wishful thinking? Or would time work to ease the uncertainty that filled her? To erase the feelings and emotions that always rose so strongly when she thought about Sam?

Bill scrambled up the small set of bleachers, shaded by a flapping canvas tarp high overhead. Lisa climbed up behind him, glancing around once more to see if she could spot Sam. There were dozens of men milling around. A woman here and there showed the growing change in ranching, which was still predominantly a man's world.

No sign of Sam. She wasn't sure if she was disappointed or not.

The auction went smoothly at least Lisa thought it did. Most of her attention was focused inward. On seeing Sam again and the emotions that churned since he'd spoken her name. Instant heat had flooded through her. Then a vague yearning.

Now fear grew. How serious was he about requesting more time with Joey? She loved her son, wanted to protect him against all of life's hurt and disappointments. And she for sure didn't want him growing up as suspicious and distrusting as his father.

But how could she fight the Hallers? Their ranch was prosperous in an era when more and more ranches were folding. Their roots went as deep in Texas soil as her own. And Sam hadn't fled the scene as she had. He had a solid background while she had lived in three different places in two years and had a total of $173 in savings.

Blindly, she stared at the bull being paraded in front of the crowd waiting to bid for it. She tuned out the drone of the auctioneer.

Instead, the years faded and she was that naive twenty-two year old who'd been so crazy about Sam Haller, she'd thrown caution to the wind and pursued him until he married her. She'd been dumb, foolish and stupid. All the things she hoped she'd learned from and wouldn't repeat if she ever decided to take a chance on a relationship again.

But the hurt from their divorce was too strong even after two years. She hadn't dated in that time. Devoting herself to her baby, she'd found contentment in making a home for Joey, and in finding out she could earn a living and become a respected member of the adult world on her own.

If she had a magic wand, however, she'd go back and change things. Change herself. Maybe even change the outcome of her marriage.

"The one we want is up next," Bill said, almost bouncing on the bench.

Lisa smiled, trying to bring herself into the present. She

owed her employer her full attention. She was lucky to get this job. To find a nice apartment in Fort Worth, only two hours from Tumbleweed. Her parents were thrilled hoping to see more of Joey, their first and so far, only grandchild.

If her sister didn't marry, Joey would end up being their only grandchild forever, she thought sadly.

When she'd first married Sam, she'd planned on a half dozen boys and girls. She'd wanted to fill that rambling old house of his with laughter and joy.

Instead, they fought like cats and dogs.

She wished she could blame him as she had when filing. But with the years apart had come maturity and the knowledge she'd been equally at fault.

The only purely happy times were when they had been in bed. And she didn't dwell on those times it hurt too much to know she wouldn't ever have anything like it again.

Sam had been the sexiest man she'd ever known. That hadn't changed. And she'd felt like a different person when he focused that blatant male attention on her. His kisses had been pure bliss. His touch had inflamed her instantly.

Thinking about it had her bothered all over again. She shifted on the bleacher and tried to focus on the sale in progress.

Get a grip, she told herself.

Seeing him had upset her.

And started her hormones dancing. She needed to concentrate on the threat of his taking Joey, not imagining him reaching out to kiss her, touch her, drive her to the heights of delight with his mouth and hands and body.

Had coming back to Texas been a mistake? Should she have kept her distance and stayed in Denver? No use second guessing things now. She'd made the move and she planned to stay in Texas.

She'd been so homesick, so lonely away from family and

friends in Denver. She'd grown up since leaving. She could handle whatever life threw her way now. She was staying in Texas.

And somehow she'd figure out a way to deal with Sam and Joey and all the problems that arose between divorced people who both loved their child.

One week later , Sam Haller pulled his pickup over to the curb and stopped. This was the place. He gazed at the brick building through the windshield. It didn't look like much, but then he reckoned costs were higher in Fort Worth than Tumbleweed. Maybe the apartments were spacious. But from the size of the small windows, and how closely placed they were, he doubted it.

He sat in the silent truck, studying the neighborhood. He wasn't expected. Would she even be home? It had taken three days for his attorney to obtain her current address. Sam waited impatiently each one of those days. He'd wanted to jump in the pickup and head for Fort Worth the minute he had the address. But he'd waited to see if she'd make any response to the letter his attorney sent.

He hadn't heard a word. Today his patience ran out.

Tugging on his Stetson, he climbed out of the truck. How could she choose this glass and brick complex over her family's place in Tumbleweed? No trees, no space, even the air seemed clogged with automobile fumes.

Nothing like the sweet smells of open range hay drying in the summer sun, or the familiar pungent scent of cattle. The sun shone through a haze, not from a clear sky so blue it almost hurt the eyes.

Heading to the large double glass doors that led into the apartment building, Sam noticed the tiny grassy area in front.

The long asphalt driveway that led behind the structure to the parking lot didn't offer any hope of more grass in back. Looking up the street again he noticed more of the same brick buildings, few trees and little grass. Two trees up the road looked substantial, otherwise, nothing worth noting. Heck of a place for a little boy to grow up.

Of course if he got his way, Joey'd spend at least half his life on the ranch. He'd grow up on the clean open spaces, learn to deal with cattle and horses and the various aspects of nature that went into running a successful cattle enterprise. He'd have his own horse and his own place on the ranch. It was where his son belonged.

Sam took a deep breath and headed inside. Not that living on a ranch was any guarantee of happiness. He'd proved that with his own life.

Lisa's apartment was on the second floor. He bypassed the elevator to take the stairs. Apartment 21 was a corner unit. He doffed his Stetson, ran his fingers through his hair and pressed the doorbell.

Nothing but silence.

He guessed he shouldn't have expected to her be home. It was still early on a Thursday afternoon. She was probably somewhere off helping Bill Taylor become a success. He frowned. She could have had a job at his spread, if she wanted to work on a ranch so much.

He almost laughed at that. She couldn't wait to shake the dust of Tumbleweed from her heels when she left. Working for him would be the last thing she'd ever want.

Still the thought wouldn't go away.

Where was Joey? At some day care center? Blast it, he didn't like the thought. He ran his fingers through his hair again and replaced his hat. He'd have to come back later. But he wasn't going home until he saw her.

Turning, he debated what to do next. He didn't know Lisa's schedule. Not that he needed to. He'd come to see his son, not learn the details of his ex-wife's new life.

The sound of a chain scrapped across the door. It opened a crack.

"Sam?" Lisa croaked.

Sam turned back. The woman peering up at him couldn't be the same one he'd seen a week ago. This one looked like something the cat dragged in. Eyes red-rimmed and bloodshot, hair lank and hanging around her face, her skin looked the color of day-old bread dough.

Shocked, Sam stared. "Are you all right? You look awful!"

She shook her head and leaned wearily against the edge of the door.

"No, of course I'm not all right," she croaked. "I have the worst case of flu in the history of the world. What are you doing here?"

"I came to see Joey."

"He isn't home. Go away, Sam." She began to shut the door.

His boot stopped it from closing.

"Open up and let me inside. You look as if you could use some help. Where's Joey? Is he sick, too?"

"No. He's at the neighbors. If you're here about the custody letter your lawyer sent, I'm not up to battling you today. When I'm better, I'll fight, but not today. Go away."

"Open the door, Lisa."

Ignoring her directive, he knew she needed help. There'd be time enough later for her to get in fighting form before they had the discussion he came for.

But right now she needed help. And it looked like he was the only one around to provide it.

At the least, he could take care of Joey.

Fumbling with the chain, she released it and turned away, stumbling as she walked down a short hallway, reaching out to the wall to steady herself. The robe she wore wasn't one he remembered. And he'd definitely have remembered a terry cloth covering.

Lisa had always been pretty as a picture and usually dressed to show off her sexy figure. He hadn't thought she knew terry cloth was used for anything but towels.

He glanced around the apartment when he entered, noting the toys scattered on the floor, plastic horses and cowboys and Indians, coloring books. A newspaper lay on one end table, sections trailing to the carpet. Through the archway into the kitchen, he saw dishes stacked on the counter.

More proof she was ill. Lisa always kept an immaculate home.

The place was tiny. He felt he could touch every wall by standing in the center of the room. It was nothing like his house--the huge old family place where he rattled around all alone. Sometimes he wandered upstairs to stand in the door to the nursery. An empty room that echoed with the sound of his infant son but now remained vacant most of the year.

He noticed the pictures of Joey from the time he was an infant until his most recent photo. She'd put them everywhere--on the end table, the bookshelves, on the walls.

Captivated, Sam studied them, noting sadly how fast his boy was growing.

He felt a pang deep inside at all he was missing as his son grew up without him.

He hadn't come to make trouble, unless fighting for equal time with his child caused Lisa trouble. If she'd stayed in Tumbleweed, they could have worked something out. Alternated weeks or weekends. Something. He'd fight her on this. And he had a good chance of winning.

At least he had until recently.

Now he wasn't so sure.

He shook his head, wishing he could change the past. But it'd forever remain a futile hope. Every convoluted problem and circumstance.

Tossing his hat on the sofa, he headed down the hall to where she'd disappeared.

Lisa crawled into her bed and pulled the covers over her head. She felt wretched. The bed cradled her aching body but gave no relief. No matter how she tossed and turned, she still felt achy, miserable, sick.

And now Sam showed up.

What was he doing here? Why did he have to show up today of all days?

Maybe she imagined him. Maybe her fever spiked and she was hallucinating.

Closing her eyes, she sought the oblivion of sleep. If she could just get some rest, she'd bounce back. She had to. She had a job to attend to. And someone had to take care of Joey. Whoever designed motherhood should have made sure sickness wasn't included until children were in high school and able to fend for themselves.

She tried to remember if her mother had ever been sick when she was a child.

It wouldn't have mattered. Her father had been around and her older sister Sally and aunts and uncles and cousins galore. She'd been surrounded by family and friends in Tumbleweed. Now she had only herself to depend upon. Joey had only his mother.

No, that wasn't right. Sam was here.

"Lisa?"

The familiar husky voice danced across her nerves. For an instant memories burst forth unrestrained. Her heart raced and she almost gave into the delight that voice brought. It was the flu. It had obviously fried all her brain cells. She lowered the covers slightly and glared at the man standing in the doorway.

No one on God's green earth had the right to look so good. She groaned and covered her head again. He was as tall as she remembered maybe taller, broad shouldered and muscular. His skin looked healthy and tanned. From working outside so much, she knew. Most cowboys looked terrific, their work demanding physical stamina and honing muscles to perfection.

But they all didn't have to be so drop-dead gorgeous. Or so sexy. Or so black-hearted.

17

Two

"Go away. Go away and let me die in peace," she groaned, turning on her side, hoping the apparition would vanish.

"When was the last time you ate?" Sam asked.

"I can't keep food down. Even the thought makes me queasy."

It looked as if it weren't an apparition but the real thing.

"Some juice, then. Or tea. What would you like?"

"I'd like to be left alone."

She hated this. She hadn't seen the man for more than a few moments at a time in two years and he shows up the day she was sure she was dying. Why couldn't he have come last week, right after seeing her at the stockyard?

Or next week when she was bound to be back on her feet and ready to face the world?

"Where's Joey?" Sam asked.

"I told you, at the neighbors. Go away."

"Is Joey staying there over night?"

Sam stepped into the room. Even to Lisa it felt warm and stuffy. Would he get sick breathing the same air?

She shook her head, then realized he wouldn't be able to see her under the covers. Great move, Lisa, she thought.

Where was all that maturity she'd so painstakingly built up

over the last twenty-four months?

"No. He'll be back later this afternoon," she replied.

"You aren't worried about getting him sick?"

"Yes, that's why he's there."

"And when he gets home?"

She flung back the covers and glared at him. "I'll deal with it, all right? Just get out."

"I'm not going anywhere."

His calm tone angered her even more. As did his casual posture leaning against the door frame, his arms crossed across his chest.

She sighed, too tired to fight. Sam was the world's most stubborn man. If he planned to stay, there was nothing she could do to dislodge him. Not until she felt better.

Which at the rate she was going might be never.

She closed her eyes and heard his tread as he walked away. The boots sounded muffled on the carpet. It'd been a long time since she'd heard boots in her home.

A wave of homesickness washed through her. She missed Tumbleweed. Missed her friends and neighbors, and the cowboys and ranchers who worked in the community. Missed her mother. She hadn't known it would be so hard to live away from her family, away from everything she loved.

Most of all she'd missed Sam.

She should have returned to Tumbleweed when she'd left Denver. Fort Worth wasn't home.

She knew why Sam'd come and wished he'd chosen his time better.

He was here about the custody suit. And after seeing her like this, he'd have even more ammunition for his side. She was all alone in Fort Worth, with only neighbors--practically strangers-- to rely on for help.

He'd only have to point out he lived in the house his family had owned for generations, a legacy for his son. His brother lived on the ranch property and would be available to help care for the boy if Sam became incapacitated.

Not to mention the ranch hands and long time family friends.

She groaned and turned over to her side, pulling the pillow over her head. She didn't want to think about that now.

Those wild Haller boys, the most trouble the town had ever seen, and she'd been crazy about both of them at one time or another.

But the past was all mixed up. She wanted it to go away. Wished it could be changed. Wanted to demonstrate to everyone that she was grown up now and capable of managing her own life.

Mostly she wanted to get better!

Not for the first time she wondered if leaving Tumbleweed had been such a great idea. Another mistake in a long line of them, she thought, feeling sorry for herself. Maybe she should consider admitting that and moving back.

"I made some tea. You need something to drink so you don't get dehydrated," Sam said, crossing to the bed.

"I won't keep it down," she said, swallowing hard.

It would be nice to sip something warm and then try to sleep again. Tears threatened. She'd been alone for so long. Sam's bringing her tea touched her heart.

"Try the tea. I found your aspirin, too. You're sure this is just the flu, you don't have something else? Have you seen a doctor?"

Struggling to sit up, Lisa nodded. "It's the flu. I think I caught it at the stockyard last week. At the auction there was a man coughing really hard."

He held his palm open with the aspirin. She took the pills, conscious of the calluses on his hands as her fingertips brushed lightly. Sam always worked hard, she had to give him credit for that.

Though she wished she could blame him for everything.

"Thanks," she mumbled as she took the fragrant brew. Sipping slowly, she realized he'd made sure it was the right temperature to drink immediately.

Darn the man, just when she wanted to throw the cup at him, he has to go and do something nice.

It reminded her of other nice things he'd done for her. Fixing her breakfast in bed, taking her dancing when he'd been tired from a full day's work on the range.

She blinked, resolving not to give into tears!

Sipping slowly, she became aware of his gaze. Raising her own to meet his, she tried to glare at him.

But she felt sad and knew it was probably reflected in her expression. Better that than the fear that simmered beneath the surface since seeing him last week.

"Why did you come today?" she asked.

He sat gingerly on the edge of her bed. The bed she'd bought when she first moved out. It was a double, nothing like the massive king-size bed they'd shared when married.

With Sam only a few inches away, she wished she'd bought a huge one, to maintain more distance.

"I came to see Joey," he said slowly. "Good thing I did, with you sick and all. I'm taking him home with me."

"No! You can't do that!"

"And you're going to stop me?"

Tears swam in her eyes. He knew she couldn't do anything not today.

"It's best for him, don't you think?" Sam asked.

If she let herself think at all, she'd have to admit he was right. But she hated to have her son gone. She hated the visits he'd made to see Sam over the last two years--missed him so much each time.

Reluctantly she had to agree Joey would be better off away from her while she was sick.

"I guess. But only until I'm better."

He looked at her dispassionately. "Maybe you should come to the ranch, too, until you're better. Who's going to look after you?"

"No." She couldn't go back. "Besides, that'd infect everyone there. I can manage myself."

He stood and paced the small room, glancing at her from time to time.

He stopped at the foot of the bed, indecision clearly evident.

"There's something else you probably should know. You'll find out sooner or later."

Her heart skipped a beat and then began to race. The headache she'd begun fighting two days ago bloomed and she closed her eyes.

He was getting married again. He'd found another woman to share his life with.

Her heart skipped a beat, then blood pounded through her veins. She felt sick and didn't think it had to do with the flu.

She wasn't ready for this.

Another thought struck her. Sam's being married would make it even more appealing to a judge when deciding Joey's custody. Sam would be able to provide a normal two-parent family like every child deserved.

While she was a single mother, far from family and a support network. Tears slipped beneath her lids and slid down her cheek.

"Hey, Lisa, are you worse?" Sam moved swiftly to her side, brushing away the tears and steadied the tea cup in her hand.

She shook her head, and opened her eyes, feeling like a fool. "I feel rotten, but no worse. You'll get it, Sam, if you hang around."

"I'm tough." He looked at her for a moment, then looked away. "About what I want to tell you," he began.

"I don't want to hear it," she snapped.

He looked at her. "What?"

"If it's bad enough for you to come to tell me in person after the way we parted, it has to be awful and I'm not up to hearing awful news."

Come back in a decade, or two.

She drained the cup and handed it to him. "Thanks for the tea. No chance of your leaving, is there?"

Slowly Sam shook his head. "I'm staying until Joey gets home. Then we'll get out of your way. Unless you want me to stay and take care of you."

"You can't stay here!" she said quickly.

She absolutely could not deal with Sam in her apartment for another few minutes, much less the day or two that it might take for her to recover.

He frowned. "Then I'll take Joey home with me. When you're well, you can come and get him."

"No."

"It's not open for discussion. I'm his father. If you can't watch him, I can."

"Don't you have work to do? The ranch doesn't run by itself."

Sam frowned and looked at the empty cup. "That's part of what I want to tell you."

Imagination proved worst then the truth, Lisa decided, as her mind came up with scenario after scenario each more convoluted then the previous one. Had he lost the ranch? Was he already married? Did he have a life-threatening disease? What?

"All right, say what you came to say. Then maybe you'll leave."

"Nick is capable of running the ranch. I'm cutting back."

"Cutting back? On what? I don't understand. You never took time off. We were lucky to have a weekend in San Antonio when we got married."

"Yeah, well, things are different now. I've run the place since Dad died. Nick's taken a more active interest now."

She looked away at the sound of his brother's name. The old memories still had the power to cause strong regrets. But times changed and she was no longer the same high school girl who had once thought she loved Nick Haller.

That had ended long ago.

Not that Sam believed it.

She'd made such a mess of things. But she'd learned and moved on. There'd been no other choice.

"Good for Nick."

Sam grinned at her. Lisa's heart almost stopped.

That sexy, lopsided grin reminded her of everything that had gone wrong in her life. The way she felt when he smiled at her about melted her bones. Her breath caught and she looked away lest she gave him ideas into her thoughts. Darn it all, they'd been divorced for two years, she had no feelings left for the man.

Except anger.

And dislike.

And resentment.

And...she stopped thinking. It was safer to just ignore him. Or ignore him as much as she could. He wouldn't stay forever. Once he took Joey, she'd be able to forget him until she was well.

"The thing is, Lisa, Nick's getting married."

She stared at him. The man Sam thought she still cared about was getting married? Closing her eyes, she waited for a reaction.

None came, unless she counted a twinge of relief. *It wasn't Sam getting married!*

Opening her eyes, she stared at him. Stared into the dark blue eyes that watched her so cautiously. Startled to see the concern in his gaze, she quickly asked, "Who to?"

"Her name is Jennifer Carson. She's from Virginia."

"Virginia? He's marrying some woman from Virginia? How in the world did he meet her?"

"At a horse show last summer. She moved to Tumbleweed in January. She's teaching elementary school in town. Hits the horse shows on the side. She has a beautiful bay gelding you'll love to see in action."

Lisa stared at Sam, disbelief warring with incredulity.

Wild, willful, sexy Nick Haller marrying a *school teacher?*

Unbelievable!

Almost as unbelievable as it had been when Sam Haller married her, she thought, staring at the man who'd been her husband for two tumultuous years. The man who'd fathered her child.

Suddenly she felt exhausted. Her head hurt and she wanted to be alone.

"You don't seem to mind," Sam said.

"I believe I told you at least a hundred times, I don't love Nick. You were the one who'd never believe that."

"You didn't act like you were over him two years ago."

"You misread the situation as I also tried to explain a hundred times!"

Scooting down in the bed, she rested her head against the

pillow. "My head still hurts and I don't feel so good. Maybe the tea was a mistake."

"Lie quietly for a while and see if your stomach settles. Tell me where Joey is and I'll go get him."

"He'll want to play with Kevin a bit longer. It's apartment 39, up one floor. But let him stay. Rosie will bring him down around four."

Lisa wanted him to leave, but once he'd left the bedroom, perversely she wished he'd stayed. Wished he'd told her more about Nick and his forthcoming marriage. Told her about the situation at the ranch. And told her what she could expect from him with this custody battle.

She couldn't stand to lose her son. Why did Sam start this? He hadn't done much with Joey when he was smaller. Of course he'd been a baby and Sam had to work. She'd left him even before Joey could walk. For a moment she tried to imagine what it would be like to have Joey live with Sam for six months each year. She'd miss so much of his growing up.

Like Sam had? a voice whispered.

Sam rinsed the cup and then ran water on the dishes. How long has she been sick? There were the remnants of at least two meals in the sink. Gazing out the small window over the kitchen sink, he didn't notice the parking garage, nor the row of brick apartment buildings beyond. He was still in her room, seeing the surprise in her eyes when he told her about Nick.

And not seeing the devastation he expected.

Was she truly over his brother?

Not that it mattered. Just because he no longer loved Nick didn't mean he and Lisa had anything. Their past was too bitter to go down that road again.

And there was another major complication that would never go away.

But for a long moment he wished that he'd handled things differently. That he hadn't been a complete idiot from beginning to end.

One of his biggest regret was he let Joey go without a monumental fight.

At first, he thought the baby should be with his mother. And he'd expected Lisa to stay in Tumbleweed.

As time went on, he knew he needed to be a bigger part of Joey's life. To teach his son, to watch him grow, to be there for him as Sam's father hadn't been for Sam.

Nothing like a bad role model to show a man how to parent.

He'd made his share of bad mistakes--Margot being the biggest. Though he had once laid that also at Lisa's door, it was his fault from start to finish. It was time to make amends where he could.

Maybe he and Lisa could find a way to build a truce for Joey's sake.

Sam glanced at his watch. It was mid afternoon. If he got Joey now, they'd be home by dinner. He went exploring. The apartment was tiny, but had three bedrooms. Each smaller than the last. The smallest Lisa had turned into an office.

At least her job enabled her to be with Joey. He remembered how angry he'd been when he heard his son was spending long hours in day care in Denver while Lisa worked. Had that been one reason she'd accepted this position?

Entering Joey's room, he paused for a moment savoring the room. Toys cluttered the floor. Picture books lay scattered near a shelf. Pajamas lay across the end of the bed. Glancing around, he noticed a photograph in the table by Joey's pillow. It was of him and Lisa in happier times.

He strode over and picked it up. At least she kept a likeness of him around so Joey wouldn't forget him. But it wasn't enough. He wanted his son to know him not just what he looked like.

Quickly he packed enough clothes to last a few days. He'd pick up Joey and head back to the ranch.

He hesitated outside Lisa's bedroom door. Should he leave her alone sick as she was? Would the neighbors check in once in a while?

Peering in, he saw she was asleep. Probably the best thing for her.

In less than ten minutes he was letting himself back into her apartment, Joey at his side. They'd grab his bag, tell Lisa goodbye and head out.

There was a familiar sound coming from the bathroom.

"Mommy's sick," Joey said leaning his head to one side to peer down the hall. "She's been sick a long time."

"Stay right here." Sam put him on the sofa and hurried down the hall to push open the bathroom door.

"You're coming home with me," he said, reaching down to draw her to her feet.

"I can't," she said, leaning against him weakly.

"You can and will."

They'd still make dinner, Sam thought with some satisfaction as he turned into the long access road that led to his home. Lisa protested about coming but he'd won the point, he thought with some satisfaction, glancing at her.

She was still asleep, leaning against the window. If he'd known he was bringing them both home, he'd have brought a car instead of the pickup.

He flicked a quick look at Joey, who stared fascinated out

the windshield from his car seat in the center.

"Cows," he said, pointing to a small herd near the fence.

"Cattle. Steers, to be accurate," Sam corrected.

Joey grinned at him. "Where are horses?"

"There'll be plenty of horses. Do you want to go riding with me?"

Joey nodded delightedly, clapping his hands.

They drove round the bend and Nick's house came into view. Once the foreman's place, Nick appropriated it when he moved out of the family house several years ago.

As he always did, Sam tried to ignore the structure as he drove past, and the memories of his last blasting accusations. The angry, hateful words that'd ended his marriage.

In another half mile they'd reach the main house. He ran a practiced eye over the fences lining the road, then checked the grass--still green and thick from the winter rain. He was cutting back on the management, allowing his brother to take a bigger role.

But some habits would never die. And owning fifty-one percent of the family ranch meant the final responsibility would always fall to him.

When the house came into view, Sam studied it a moment, wondering what Lisa would think.

He'd spent the greater part of their first summer apart scraping, sanding and painting the place after he'd done his stint on the range each day. He'd needed the task to keep him from going crazy. Then he'd fall into bed with a bottle. A bad habit that'd cost him.

Stopping by the front porch, he cut the engine and released Joey from his car seat.

"Okay, partner, let's get your mommy settled and you and I'll go check out the horses."

"Yippee!"

Joey flung his arms around Sam's neck and hugged him tightly.

Sam swung him out of the truck and set him on the ground. "Stay with me until you get acquainted, now," he admonished.

He took the suitcases from the truck bed and headed into the house. He had to make up a bed for Lisa. She could sleep in the pickup until it was ready, then he'd come and get her.

Before he had the guestroom bed fully made, however, he heard her run into the house and slam the downstairs bathroom door behind her.

"Oh-oh, looks like your mom didn't make it," he said to Joey, flicking on a light blanket. The youngster reached over to pull it up to the pillow.

"I'll go get your mom," Sam said, heading down the stairs an odd sense of anticipation building.

He waited until she slowly opened the door, then scooped her up and carried her up to bed over her protests. He hesitated a split second before the opened door to their room. The one they'd shared when married. But he'd forfeited the right to have her there.

The guest room would do until she was fit again.

"I don't want to be here," she complained as he and Joey settled her in the bed.

"Noted."

"Get better, Mommy," Joey said, patting her shoulder.

"Okay, honey. I'll get better fast." She glared up at Sam. "As soon as I can!"

He grinned at that. "I'm sure this is the best medicine--staying here will insure you'll get better as fast as you can."

Turning her head away, she made no response.

"Come on, partner, let's get some chow," Sam said, holding his hand out for Joey. "We'll check in on you when we get back from dinner."

Lisa said nothing as she listened to the two of them walk away. Closing her eyes, she tried to find some relief. She was so miserable.

And not the least was being back in Sam's house when she'd rather be anywhere else.

Memories flooded and she tried to keep them at bay. She didn't want to remember anything good about those years. Or about Sam.

Maybe she'd call her mother in the morning and see if she could go home. Anything would be better than staying here.

The only good aspect was she didn't have to worry about Joey. No one would take better care of him than his dad.

In the morning, Lisa changed her mind. Sam checked on her twice in the night, bringing her warm tea and making sure she was holding down the liquids. The nausea had faded. Now she was just bone weary.

Maybe she'd call her mother in another day or so.

Sam hated seeing Lisa sick. She'd been in robust health all the time he'd known her. And radiant while pregnant.

He called the doctor first thing that morning, but was told there was nothing he could do that Sam wasn't already doing. It was a matter of time.

He took Joey with him when doing chores, showing him around the ranch again, amazed at what the little boy remembered from his last visit several months ago.

Nick drove up to the barn at eight. He alighted from his truck, spotting Joey and grinned.

"Hey, Joey, I didn't know you were coming to visit! How you doing?"

Sam watched as Joey flew across the yard to jump up into Nick's embrace.

He tried to ignore the twinges of jealousy that poked. His brother hadn't cheated with Lisa. They'd both told him so over and over.

He believed them. But it had taken a long time.

He still felt irritated at how easily Nick got on with everyone. For Sam it was a struggle. He knew his more distant nature was a direct result of dealing with their father, but it didn't make it easier.

Might as well get it all over with.

"Lisa's here, too," he said, ambling over to Nick.

Nick looked surprised, his glance flicking to the front of the old house.

"Here, as in a visit?"

"Sort of. She's sick."

Nick put Joey down and looked at his brother. "How sick?"

"She has the flu. There wasn't anyone to take care of Joey, so I brought him here. She's so sick, I brought her, too."

"You brought her here? After all she did? Are you nuts?"

"No. I thought you might be glad to see her again," Sam said.

Nick's grin cut off and he narrowed his eyes. "Just what is that supposed to mean?"

"We're going riding, Unca Nick," Joey said brightly. "Me and Daddy."

"Good for you, sport. You have fun." Nick responded to Joey, but his gaze never left Sam's.

"Let it mean whatever you want."

Sam looked at Joey, knowing he should have kept his mouth shut. Baiting his brother wasn't the way he wanted things.

"I'll be glad to see her, but that's all. Are you forgetting Jennifer?" Nick asked.

Sam shook his head.

"Come on, Joey, let's saddle up."

Nick turned back to his truck to pull some baling wire from the back. "Dang fool thing to do, if you ask me," he mumbled.

Sam headed for the barn, distracted by Joey's wild enthusiasm about riding. Next time he'd keep his mouth shut.

They'd had their problems, but had worked through most of them. Bringing Lisa to the ranch just brought everything up again.

The past was hard to ignore. And the suspicions and the hurt the hardest to end.

By Friday, Lisa was going crazy. She felt much better, was eating scrambled eggs and soup and keeping everything down.

But Sam wouldn't hear of her getting up. Or at least not when he was home.

As soon as he and Joey left that morning, she rose and took a shower. Making the bed with fresh sheets, she crawled thankfully back beneath the covers a half hour later. Feeling tired, but clean and fresh again, she acknowledged that maybe it was too early to get up and resume her normal routine.

But the ranching magazines Sam brought her didn't hold her interest.

Idly, she began to wonder if any of the novels she'd had were still around. Or had he gotten rid of them when he'd sent her things to her mother's?

The ranch cook brought her soup at lunch. After eating most of the bowlful, Lisa felt restless. She took the empty bowl downstairs. Someone from the big kitchen at the bunkhouse could pick it up later. Sam obviously took his meals with the cowboys now that she wasn't here to cook for him.

Dinners had been the highlight of her day. Especially if he'd take her out. She experimented with different concoctions most nights, but loved eating out.

That has sure changed in the last two years. First of all, a small child wasn't conducive to quiet dining. And her finances had been too limited to splurge on something as unnecessary as an expensive meal when she could prepare something herself that was just as tasty.

Wandering slowly around the first floor, Lisa was fascinated to note the changes. She'd expected everything to remain the same.

He'd bought a new sofa for the front room, upholstered in browns and cream. The scarred coffee table was still in place, lending a familiar touch.

The large screen TV was new. They hadn't watched a lot of television.

Did Sam fill his evening that way now? Was he as lonely as she sometimes felt?

Or did he hang out with his ranch hands at the chow hall until time for bed?

She'd remembered their evenings. They'd gone dancing, visiting with friends, picnicking on the escarpment that overlooked the ranch.

When he wasn't accusing her of making a play for Nick, or acting childish, or ignoring the demands of the ranch, that was.

One thing she'd say for her marriage, it'd been full of passion--passionate fighting, and passionate making-up.

She crossed the room to the bookcase quickly scanning the titles. Choosing a mystery she hadn't read, she was saddened to notice none of her books remained.

Had he purged the house of all traces of her?

And why not, she asked herself as she headed back up stairs. She'd wanted the relationship to end. She'd done her best to erase every aspect of Sam from her life. It was only fair to expect him to do the same.

Passing the master bedroom, she paused in the doorway. The big bed sat in the same spot centered against the long wall, the huge dresser with the deep drawers on the adjacent wall.

She missed all that space in her apartments.

"Lisa?" Sam said behind her.

She jumped and turned. How had he come up the stairs without her hearing him?

"What are you doing?"

"I didn't hear you," she said, taking a deep breath to settle her nerves. Only it didn't settle anything. She drew in his scent, fresh and clean like the wide open spaces of the ranch with a hint of horse and leather.

It was said smell was one of the strongest triggers for memories. It must be true, a million crowded instantly in her mind.

Three

"What are you doing?" Sam repeated, glancing beyond her into the bedroom, his expression enigmatic.

"Nothing. I went to get something to read beside the magazines you brought up. I wanted something entertaining, not educational."

She held up the mystery, trying to ignore the guilty feeling that swept through her. She had no business staring into their room. The last thing she wanted was for Sam to think she wanted to go in.

Sam's room, not their room.

"Are you feeling better?" he asked politely.

She nodded, realizing how much the trek downstairs had taken out of her. She looked away, ready to head back to the guest room, trying to quell the memories that filled her.

She remembered when he'd come in from working, sweep her into his arms and kiss her breathless. Then carry her into their bedroom and shut the door firmly behind them.

She'd loved it when he'd come in unexpectedly during the day just to see her, complaining it'd been too long since he'd last kissed her.

Had she ever told him how exciting that was?

The poignant memory caught her unaware. She turned away from temptation, away from sad memories and headed down the hall toward the guest room. She had no business staying in Sam's house. The sooner she left, the better it'd be for all.

"Lisa?" Sam called.

She turned. He hadn't moved, still stood by the door watching her with that unreadable expression.

"I'm taking Joey on a ride. I came to see if you needed anything before we go."

She shook her head.

"Where's Joey now?" she asked.

"Helping Jose soap some leather."

Sam's expression softened and he almost smiled.

Lisa felt the catch in her breath. She could look at him all day! Shouldn't she be beyond this fluttering feeling?

Where was the anger she'd felt so explosively two years ago?

The hurt of his accusations?

The feelings of abandonment that had seemed so strong when he had cut back on their dinners in town claiming ranch work came first?

"He might want to change his name," he said.

"What?"

"He found out Jose is Spanish for Joe, so now he's saying he wants to be called Jose."

Lisa smiled. Sometimes Joey had the oddest take on things.

Sam frowned. "If you're okay, I'll head back. I don't pay the men to be babysitters."

He turned and descended the stairs. Lisa wondered why the sudden change in mood. She hadn't asked him to come check on her.

For a moment she almost called after him. To say what? Thanks for checking up on me? Want to talk?

Surprised at the thought, she hurried into her room. There

was nothing left to talk about. Hadn't they talked at each other for months?

And, of course, that had been the problem. They'd talked at each other, neither taking the time to really listen.

Sam crossed the yard with long strides. He hadn't needed to go inside to see Lisa. Pete said he'd checked on her when he took the soup he'd made especially for her.

But she was a guest in his household. He'd have done the same with any visitor.

But he wouldn't have reacted to any other visitor's smile like he did to Lisa's. He'd felt it to his toes. His body tightening, his blood heating up in a flash. He didn't liked that reaction at all.

Scowling, he headed for the barn. He'd get Joey and take off for the northwest boundary. No one had been up there in a few days and it didn't pay to ignore the miles of fencing for long. Cattle had a way of pushing through at the most inconvenient time.

The ride would be good for both of them.

"Lisa doing okay?" Nick asked, leading a saddled horse from the barn.

Sam nodded, the old memories surging despite his attempts to keep them locked down.

At least he didn't have to give way to them. The uneasy relationship he'd had with his brother was slowly solidifying. He wouldn't let anything damage that fragile trust.

"Did you remember Jennifer's coming this afternoon as soon as school's out to discuss the wedding reception?" Nick asked.

"I remember," Sam said. "Do you really need me here?"

"She wants you involved."

Nick slapped the end of the reins into the palm of one hand. "She doesn't have any brothers or sisters and this is her way to, um, bond with you. She wants your input for the reception since you said we could have it here on the ranch."

"I haven't changed my mind. The main house and yard will easily hold the whole town, if you're going to invite them."

"She just may."

"I'll be back around four."

"Think Lisa will still be here?" Nick said.

"I haven't heard she's planning to leave this afternoon. Why?"

Sam heard the sharp tone in his voice. It was instinctive, not intentional.

"Just wondered. Pete said she was up this morning."

Nick turned to mount his horse. Settling in the saddle, he looked down at his brother, leaning over and resting a forearm on the saddle horn.

"Lisa's the mother of my nephew. If you get to have Joey here half the year, Jennifer will see a lot of him. Might as well meet his mother, I guess."

Sam shrugged. "We'll see."

"Where are you heading?" Nick asked.

"I'm taking Joey for a ride up by the Parkerson's boundary. He likes riding and we can check that stretch of fencing at the same time."

Nick eased back in the saddle, reset his hat. "I'm going to the bore. One of the hands said the windmill was screeching. I want to see for myself before ordering repairs."

Sam nodded and continued into the barn. He and his brother had worked through their conflict.

If only he and Lisa could have done so.

But she'd taken off without a backward glance. They'd never recapture the past. That door was shut.

And there were added complications now that locked the door.

He stopped in the doorway to the tack room, amused to see Joey industriously trying to help Jose with the leather work.

"Ready to go, partner?" he asked.

"Yes!" Joey came up like a shot. "I have to go, Jose. Me and Daddy're going riding," he said proudly. He loved being on the back of a horse.

Sam couldn't wait until Joey was old enough to handle his own mount. The two of them could cover the entire ranch on horseback.

As he and Lisa had done when first married.

He'd wanted to show off to her, show what she got by marrying him. She'd been interested and full of questions. Sometimes they picnicked on the escarpment, other times they explored different shady spots as lovers.

They'd even made use of one of the old line cabins one afternoon. The threatening storm had started sooner than anticipated. Rather than race home in the rain, they'd holed up in the old cabin and whiled away the afternoon. He'd often wondered if that had been when Joey had been conceived.

He shook his head. He needed to stop thinking about the past and about Lisa!

By the time Sam and Joey returned later that afternoon, Jennifer's car was parked in front of the house. Sam debated the merits of asking one of the men to take care of the horse or doing it himself. Anything to delay seeing Nick and Jennifer so happy together.

It was hard to deal with in light of the mess he'd made of his own life.

Jose ambled from the barn. "Boss," he touched the brim of his hat.

Sam lifted Joey. "Jose, would you take care of my mount?"

"Sure thing." The old Mexican cowhand reached for the reins.

"I wanted to brush him," Joey protested.

"We have company. Your uncle Nick's getting married soon to a nice lady. She's come to meet you. When she and Nick are hitched, she'll be your Aunt Jennifer."

"Why are they getting married?" Joey asked, his arms firmly around his father's neck as Sam strode to the house.

"They want to be together."

"Is she a cowboy?"

"No, she's a school teacher. But she'll live here on the ranch with Nick. She loves him and loves the ranch. And she really loves horses. She has a beauty herself."

Joey was silent a moment. Just as Sam reached the porch, he said, "Can Mommy and I live here on the ranch, too? We love it here!"

Sam glanced at Joey's shining eyes. This is where his son belonged.

"Tell you what, why don't you suggest that to your mom?"

Lisa'd probably kill him. But for the moment, he didn't care. He was glad Joey wanted to live on the spread. And he'd be interested in just what she had to say about it.

When they entered the house, Nick and Jennifer came from the kitchen, Nick carrying a tray of icy beverages. Jennifer smiled at Sam and Joey.

"Hi. And who is this? I bet you're Joey."

Joey nodded his head, shyly clutching his dad.

"I'm Jennifer."

"Aunt Jennifer," he said.

"That's right or I will be soon. I'm happy to meet you. I bet we get to be friends fast," she said with a friendly smile.

Sam set his son down and headed him toward the downstairs bathroom. "We'll wash up and join you."

Lisa leaned against the wall a few feet back from the top of the stairs. No one noticed her and she took the moment to study Jennifer and Nick before descending. She'd dressed a little while ago in jeans and a comfortable blue top. Not that she had much choice. Sam had only grabbed a few things for her when they left Fort Worth.

Her shower earlier had left her hair shiny and full of body. She'd put on a little makeup just so she didn't look so pale, she told herself.

She thought to surprise Sam by coming downstairs.

It was she who was surprised. She hadn't expected company.

Should she continue down, or return to her room? Was she up to meeting the bride?

Nick looked good--and happy. She was glad to know he'd found someone special.

Despite Sam's suspicions, she was glad Nick was so in love with someone he wanted to marry her.

They'd been high school sweethearts. Those feelings had faded, however. Not that Sam believed it.

He persisted in thinking she had a hankering for Nick.

How he could have ever thought such a thing was beyond her. He was twice the man his brother was! Twice as exciting, twice as appealing, and twice as sexy.

She should have handled things more maturely.

Lisa had a real thing about maturity these days because she felt her own behavior in the past had lacked that commodity.

Taking a deep breath, she decided to continue down the stairs.

"Mommy, Mommy, you're better!"

Joey came racing down the hall just as she reached the bottom. He flung himself around her legs and squeezed tightly.

"I'm better," she said, sitting on the bottom step and pulling him into her lap, hugging him tightly. She looked up into Sam's dark blue eyes.

"Guess what," Joey said, excitedly. "Daddy said to ask you if we can stay here! We can live here all the time, like Jennifer is gonna do. Can we, Mommy? Can we live here?"

The color left her cheeks as she looked at Sam in disbelief.

"No, we certainly can't live here! How dare you suggest such a thing!"

He shrugged as Nick came into the hall from the living room. For a moment he glanced between the two of them, then nodded.

"Lisa."

Not exactly a ringing welcome, Lisa thought. "Hi Nick."

He put his hands in the pockets of his jeans and rocked back on his boot heels, his eyes narrowed as he looked at her. Was there a hint of hostility in the air?

"You're looking better than I'd thought you'd be," he said.

"If you like pale as a ghost," Sam muttered.

Lisa ignored Sam. "I'm feeling better, just a little shaky. I hear congratulations are in order."

Nick nodded, looked around, and reached out to take Jennifer's hand as she joined them, his expression softening as he smiled at her.

"Jennifer, Lisa."

"Hi, Lisa," Jennifer said.

Lisa set Joey on his feet and slowly rose to her own. She smiled politely at Jennifer, struck at how fresh and pretty she looked. It made Lisa even more conscious of her own wan appearance.

She also noted the contrast in Nick's manner. What was going on?

"Nice to meet you, Jennifer. Best wishes for a lifetime of happiness."

Jennifer smiled happily and leaned against Nick. "Thanks. I expect to have exactly that with this guy!"

Lisa expected that as well once. Sam had been larger than life for her.

Older by five years, he'd already begun to make a mark on his newly-inherited ranch when he'd starting dating her. And with those added years had come experience enough to sweep her off her feet. She'd felt very special in those days.

It had been a long time since she'd felt special, she thought wryly.

"I fixed some lemonade," Jennifer said into the growing silence. "Does anyone want any?"

"I do," Joey said promptly, racing for the living room.

In a few minutes, everyone had moved into the large comfortable room and were seated, icy glasses in hand.

Tension shimmered in the air. Lisa looked from one brother to the other, both had their gaze on her. Were they waiting for her to say something?

Sam dominated the room. It was all she could do to concentrate on Nick and Jennifer and not stare at Sam, absorbing every nuance and expression that crossed his face.

Not that there would be many. He was a master at keeping his thoughts to himself unless he wanted others to know.

She felt warm, flushed. It couldn't be from the flu, she hadn't had a fever for a couple of days. Maybe it was the sense of awareness she experienced being around Sam again.

Why was he looking at her?

Jennifer began to speak rapidly and Lisa tried to concentrate on what she was saying.

"So, of course it's the typical June wedding. But I don't care. I only expect to get married once, so I'm doing it up just the way I want."

She glanced at Nick and smiled. "Or the way we want, I hope."

"Whatever you want, is what I want," he said with a smile.

Lisa blinked.

Had she heard the man correctly? She flicked a glance at Sam, startled to find his gaze still on her. They locked eyes for a second, sharing the moment, almost as if they shared a common thought.

Nick? Acting like a love stuck cowboy? It was mind boggling.

But nice, she thought wistfully, wishing Sam felt like that about her.

What, exactly, had he felt for her?

Passion and desire, she knew that. She'd been barely twenty-two when they'd gotten married. Now that she was almost twenty-eight, she could see she'd been too young. She hadn't finished growing up. But at the time, she'd insisted she knew what she wanted and it'd been Sam Haller.

The moment ended and she looked away, upset with the thoughts that came unbidden. They'd married fast, loved furiously, and separated after only two years.

Jennifer was speaking again, "...so since I've lost touch with so many friends since college, I thought we might as well get married here. My folks will fly in and a few close friends. And my grandparents. Otherwise, our guests will be my new friends and neighbors here in Tumbleweed."

Lisa nodded as if she'd heard the entire thing. "That's nice."

"And then we'll party here all night before leaving on our honeymoon," Jennifer finished brightly, smiling at Sam.

Lisa remembered her own wedding, small and quiet. The

brief honeymoon in San Antonio. She'd loved the Riverwalk and the Old Town and the hours spent with Sam in the hotel room.

Heat swept through her again. She dare not meet his gaze. What if he were remembering? What if the memories were unaccompanied by the same fondness?

A jarring memory surfaced unbidden--Sam's jealousy about Nick.

She still remembered his comments on their wedding night of how jealous he was of the fact she and Nick had dated. Then he'd set about to make her forget everyone she'd ever known before. And done it masterfully.

The exploits of Sam and Nick were legendary around Tumbleweed when they'd escape from their domineering father.

Even with all that had gone on between them, she remembered their lovemaking as the stuff of legends. The man had no idea how much she'd cherished their nights together.

And not only the nights. There were afternoons, mornings and everything in between. In the house, in the barn, under the open sky and once in a leaky old cabin on the edge of the ranch.

She shifted restlessly in the chair. It wasn't fair to have perfection and lose it.

"You all right?" Sam asked softly.

She looked at him, his eyes dark with concern, his attention focused on her.

Once again her heart skipped a beat, then began a rapid tempo. What would it be like to touch his cheek with her fingertips, thread her fingers through that rich dark hair, feel the remembered strength of his muscles against her softness once again? Just once.

Hadn't she heard somewhere or read in a woman's

magazine, that divorced couples sometimes got together for old times sake? Could she do that?

Would he even want another night together?

She swallowed hard, amazed where her thoughts were heading. Had her fever fried her brains?

"I'm fine," she said, startled at her husky tone.

"I'm glad you're feeling better," Jennifer said. "I hope Joey doesn't get sick. Though I'm sure the fresh air out here has been great for keeping him healthy."

"If he's missed catching it this long, I think he'll be fine," Sam said, stretching out his long legs, leaning back in the chair and crossing his arms across his chest.

"He's darling, I can see why he 'd love to live here. I bet he loves horses," Jennifer said, smiling at the little boy busy slurping the lemonade.

Lisa stiffened. "Nothing's been settled," she said sharply.

Jennifer looked at her, distressed.

"Oh, sorry, I thought..." She looked at Nick.

He shrugged, glared at Lisa.

"Lisa doesn't like the idea, but there's nothing to stop the arrangement from going through," Sam said. "Joey's old enough to begin learning about the ranch. And he likes it here, right, partner?"

Joey beamed at his father, nodding his head rapidly.

Lisa put her glass on the scarred coffee table and stood up.

"I want to talk to you," she said to Sam, conscious of Joey's sudden uncertainty as he looked between his father and mother.

"Alone and away from big ears!"

She walked quickly from the room, not waiting to see if Sam would follow.

She was seething! How dare he discuss his plans with all and sundry and in front of Joey. Especially when nothing had been settled!

Sam caught up with her in the entry, taking her arm and swinging her around.

"Hold on, Lisa. What's got you in such a twit?"

"The discussion is inappropriate!"

"What discussion? You know I'm petitioning for joint custody. It's just a matter of form."

"And you had to tell the world as if it's a done deal?"

She was finding it difficult to think coherently with his fingers on her arm. Their warmth penetrated the thin cotton sleeve, starting a tingling sensation that distracted common thought. Her skin felt too tight. The heat that swept through made her wonder if a fever was spiking.

"I told my brother, he told Jennifer hardly all and sundry. They're family."

"Until it's settled, I don't want it discussed in front of Joey."

"You heard him, he'd love to live on the ranch. He's not going to mind staying here for half the time. Heck, when he's older, he might want to live here year round."

Lisa swallowed hard, wishing he'd let her go so she could think better.

"He's only three, he doesn't know what he wants."

"Sure he does. He loves the horses, learning to ride, helping where he can. You should have seen him with Jose earlier. Don't forget a portion of the ranch will be his one day, he might as well grow up learning things, rather than inherit a place one day out of the blue like your employer did."

Nick and Jennifer came into the entry way.

"We're heading out," Nick said. "We'll catch you later about the wedding."

Jennifer looked subdued. "I'm sorry if I said something inappropriate," she said quietly, quickly moving with Nick to the door.

Lisa watched them leave. "Gee, that went well."

His fingers tightened then released her. He stepped away.

"I always thought Nick'd follow you after you left, you know," he said. "It must have been hard to see him with her."

Her gaze flew to his. "I told you we were through years ago. You're the only one who never believed it."

He shrugged. "One reason I didn't contest the divorce was I thought the two of you would be happy together. Every time you weren't where I thought you were, you were at Nick's."

He turned and headed back into the living room.

"We were friends," she called after him.

It was futile, she knew. If she had things to do over again, she'd have handled it differently.

Lisa heard him talking with Joey, wished she knew what he was telling their son. But she couldn't move.

He thought Nick would have gone after her?

Did that mean he'd have contested the divorce, not acquiesced, if he'd known his brother wasn't interested? If he had believed that she wasn't interested in Nick?

Feeling shaky, she sat on the bottom stair, trying to analyze the comment. Was there hidden meaning there? Something she should understand? Idly her fingers rubbed her arm, tracing the spot he'd touched, almost caressed.

It was past time for her to leave. She was getting in over her head.

Rising resolutely, she moved to the archway into the living room. Sam and Joey sat together on the sofa, their head bent close together, talking softly. Joey's trusting eyes were on his father, fascinated by whatever Sam was telling him.

She felt a pang. This is how it should be. Joey should be learning everything about the ranch from his father. And about manners and responsibilities and school work and everything else. He should have both parents.

Sam looked up.

"I want to go to my folks' place. Can you take me or shall I ask them to come to get me?"

"Now?"

"Now. I'll get our things together."

"Joey stays."

Sam stood up, seeming to tower over her.

She opened her mouth to argue, then closed it. "Fine, for the weekend."

"We still need to discuss things," he said slowly.

"When I'm feeling better, Sam. Not today. I just want to go home."

Wherever that was, she thought as she went upstairs to gather her few clothes. Maybe being with her parents would help her put things into perspective.

Sam and Joey were standing at the bottom of the stairs when she returned.

"I want you to consider getting a job in Tumbleweed," he said as he opened the front door. "It would be the best solution for Joey. Fort Worth is too far to travel back and forth each day. If you lived in town, when you're working, he could come here. Save child care costs and having him raised by strangers. When he's older, he can come after school, and on weekends."

"I'll think about it," she said, climbing into the pickup truck.

Joey climbed in from the driver's side, settling in his car seat. "Are we going to live here, Mommy?" he asked again. "I told Daddy we love it here."

"We'll work something out, sweetie," Lisa said, wishing she knew what it'd be.

The drive to her parent's house would have been in total silence if not for Joey's chatter. But Lisa wasn't listening.

Did Sam remember the nights he'd picked her up in the same truck? The dinners and western dancing they'd enjoyed?

The talking and laughing and loving? The passionate good night kisses? She remembered every single one and wished she didn't. Her defenses were down from being sick, she thought desperately.

When they reached her dad's house, she forced a bright smile. "Joey, want to come in and see Grandma and Grandpa?" she asked.

He shook his head. "Want to go back to the ranch," he said stubbornly.

Lisa felt a tug in her heart.

She was going to lose her son for a good part of the year, if not longer, she knew it. Her precious baby. How could she stand it?

"They'd love to see you," she said, knowing it was a lost cause, but not willing to give up easily.

"No." His expression mirrored his father's stubborn one. She felt a catch in her heart.

She looked at Sam helplessly. His expression gave nothing away.

"We do need to talk," she admitted. "But not today and not in front of Joey."

He nodded.

"We could discuss it tomorrow or the next day." She was sure to feel better by then. More able to cope.

"Come to the ranch around-- "

"No," she said quickly. "Not the ranch. Not here. Some neutral location. Lunch in town, maybe?"

"Dinner tomorrow," Sam said. "I'll get Nick to watch Joey and you and I can discuss things without the big ears."

"The sooner we settle things the sooner we can move on."

"I'll pick you up at six. We'll go to Rosie's. Is that neutral enough for you?"

A pang. Rosie's was the Tex-Mex restaurant they'd loved.

"Sounds like arms negotiations," she said to cover any hint of nostalgia.

"A truce is all I'm after," he said.

She kissed Joey, brushing her hand over his hair and feeling the ache of missing him begin. "Be good for Daddy," she said.

"Where are you going?" Joey asked, looking confused.

"I'm staying with Grandma and Grandpa tonight," she said. "You can stay with them, too, if you want."

He leaned nearer Sam. "No, I live at the ranch."

"Not live there, you're visiting."

"Give it up, Lisa, he's going to be living there sooner or later. Let him say it."

She frowned and quickly exited the truck. Sam wasn't the type to gloat, but it sure sounded like it to her.

She watched the truck disappear, feeling as if something special and sacred had disappeared with it.

She'd miss Joey she had every time he'd gone to visit Sam before. But this time there was a difference. Maybe she should have stayed one more night at the ranch.

To what end, she thought sadly, turning to open the door to her parent's house.

Had they already heard from the grapevine she was back in town? Probably not or her mother would have been on the phone in an instant.

The serenity of the old house surrounded her immediately when she stepped inside. It felt safe, secure and happy--all the attributes she associated with her childhood. Why had life turned hard as she got older?

Four

The next evening as she watched from the window of her parent's home, Lisa felt as nervous as a teenager on a first date. It wasn't as if this were a date, she reminded herself. Treaty negotiations more like.

Joey's future to discuss.

She saw the truck arrive, watched as Sam got out and headed for the front door as if he hadn't a care in the world. Wasn't he at all nervous?

Blast the man, he probably felt he held all the aces.

He knocked on the door.

"I'm going now, Mom," she called, heading for the door.

Margaret Ballantine came down the hall, wiping her hands on a kitchen towel. She was baking and the fragrance of fresh chocolate chip cookies filled the house.

"I'll speak to Sam before you go," she said.

Lisa sighed and opened the door. Twenty-seven years old and her mother had to observe the proprieties of speaking with her daughter's escort even if it was only a business meeting.

It wasn't fair, was her first thought when she opened the door. Sam looked good enough to eat. His hat rode low, his fresh shirt emphasized the breadth of his shoulders, tapering to the new jeans encasing narrow hips and long muscular legs. When his eyes met hers, she could almost feel her blood heat degree by degree. For a second it was as if they were alone in the world.

"Sam, it's been a while," Margaret said, holding out her arms.

"Margaret." He hugged her briefly.

"Bring Joey over tomorrow. I've been baking all day and can't wait to see him again. Just for the afternoon," she suggested.

Sam glanced at Lisa. "We'll see."

Five minutes later they were turning onto the highway leading to town.

"Guerrilla tactics?" he asked, smoothly blending in with the flow of traffic.

"If you mean Mom, she wants to see her grandson, that's all."

"Then it wouldn't matter to her if she had Joey at her place or if they came out to the ranch."

"I want to see Joey, too."

"You can come out as well."

Lisa sat back, pressing her lips tightly together to keep the heated words from spilling out. Was this what she could expect? She thought they were going to discuss things rationally like adults. Maybe she should start.

"I've been thinking about working from Tumbleweed. I talked to Bill today and he's agreeable to try it."

"You should have stayed here to begin with."

"Look, Sam, if you want to harp on should haves and all, then maybe this evening is pointless. I thought we were going to discuss the future, not the past."

"Right, the future." He gripped the wheel tightly.

"Anyway, I can drive out to his ranch once or twice a week, and the rest of the time do work from home, like I did in Fort Worth. If I can find an apartment for rent in town."

"Put the word out, I'm sure you'll hear of something before long. Until you get settled, Joey can stay with me."

"No."

"Sheesh, Lisa, at least give a pretense of thinking about it for a minute or two. What's wrong with him staying at the ranch?"

She couldn't tell Sam how afraid she was that Joey would continue to adore living there and become dissatisfied confined to a small apartment in town.

She didn't want to lose her son to the lure of ranching, horses, cowboys and Sam.

"He's too little," she said.

"I'm not sending him out on a roundup alone. He's having the time of his life."

"He needs his mother."

"You're going to be busy, packing up your place in Fort Worth, finding an apartment here, getting things set up, working eight hours a day. It isn't going to hurt anything for him to stay at the ranch. It'll make it easier for you."

"I don't need you making things easy for me," she snapped, her temper threatening to erupt.

Sam swerved over to the side of the road and stopped, turning to glare at her.

"I know that for darn sure. What's the real issue here?"

"I don't want Joey staying at your place."

"Why not? What's the real reason, Lisa? I'm his father."

"I don't want to be separated from my son!"

"He's my son, too, don't forget. And maybe I don't want to be separated either! You should have considered that before you walked out."

"You let me go."

"Let you? Give me a break, lady. I thought you were unhappy and wanted Nick. You both surprised the heck out of me when you didn't take up with each other again after you and I split. Especially after that last night."

"There was nothing going on with me and Nick. Nothing! As we both told you." She looked at him, her eyes narrowed. "Are you saying you were being noble and stood aside for me to find my true love?" she asked scathingly.

Sam looked away.

For a stunned moment she stared at him.

The faint hint of color in his cheeks confirmed her words. Lisa was dumbfounded.

"Oh no," she said softly.

She thought she'd cry.

Fury changed to hurt, to sadness in an instant.

He'd thought she loved his brother and had stepped aside for them.

What a waste of time, of emotions, of pain and separation.

"You did," she whispered.

"Forget it, Lisa. Don't make it out to be more tragic than it was. The issue, as you said, is the future. I want my son."

"I want him, too! I love him so much."

"And what, because I'm a man you think I don't? I made a mistake two years ago. Actually several. But this one I can rectify. I want to see as much of Joey as possible."

"What do you want from me? To just give him up? To see him on weekends, or what? What do you want from me?"

He stared at her for a long moment, then reached for her with a groan, pulling her halfway across the seat, only prevented from pulling her into his lap by her seat belt.

His mouth came down on hers. Lisa had only a split second before all rational thinking fled. His mouth was warm and firm moving against hers in a passionate kiss that reminded her of the first heady days of their marriage.

The feelings that exploded filled every cell as she moved to get closer, her arms coming around his neck. She'd have released the seat belt if she'd had enough sense. But when he deepened the kiss, she lost every speck.

Rainbow colors danced behind her closed lids. Her body heated, yearned for him. Her hands found their solace in the thick texture of his hair. Knocking his hat off, she pressed even closer. Reveling in the spiraling sensations caused when his tongue danced with hers, when his grip softened to allow his hands to roam over her back pressing her closer, she ignored the tiny hint of doubt.

This was like coming home after a long hard journey.

Her breathing became labored, but who needed oxygen? She had Sam.

At last sanity surfaced. She slowly pushed back and stared at him, dimly award his breathing was as erratic as her own. But kisses like this led to craziness.

No matter what magazines said, she couldn't continue. Not with so much unresolved between them.

What did he want? Just a kiss? Or more?

Could they recapture the past? Did either of them wish to even try?

"I'm sorry," Sam said, sitting back, reaching for his hat. He ran the fingers of one hand through his mussed hair, then carefully replaced the Stetson.

"Sorry?"

She didn't want him to regret their kiss. It'd been wonderful.

Or had it only felt wonderful for her?

He started the engine and pulled out onto the highway again. "It won't happen again," he said stiffly.

It couldn't happen again, he reminded himself after he finished calling himself every name in the book.

There was Margot.

Once Lisa found out about her, he'd be lucky if she'd even talk to him through an attorney.

What was he thinking?

He hadn't been thinking, obviously, only feeling. Feeling her softness. Breathing in the fragrance that identified her for all time. Tasting that sweet mouth. He tightened his grip on the steering wheel. He wanted her even with all that was between them. Hadn't he gotten over her in two years?

For a moment he wished he had the right to carry her off somewhere and make love all night long. Then reality hit him on the head.

That would be one dumb move. And not help his fight for his son at all.

He could feel her gaze still on him. He flicked her a glance, taking in her confused expression.

"There's no need to apologize, unless you want an apology from me as well," she said.

He shook his head. "What I want is to forget it happened. We'll be at Rosie's in a minute. You still like Mexican food?"

"Of course. Especially Tex-Mex, which was hard to find in Colorado."

He drove the rest of the way in silence. He wasn't looking forward to their discussion.

In addition to their plans for Joey, he needed to tell her about Margot before she heard about it from someone else. And they'd have to decide how to tell Joey.

He was surprised her mother hadn't already filled her in. Or maybe she had, and Lisa didn't care enough to even bring it up.

Rosie's was a popular restaurant in Tumbleweed. The cars and pickups filling the parking lot attested to the crowd they'd find inside. Maybe this wasn't such a great place to have a discussion, he thought as he pulled into a parking place. He didn't want to air his business to all and sundry.

"Looks crowded," Lisa said.

"It's Saturday night."

He stopped the engine. Before he could come around to open her door, she hopped down from the cab and headed toward the restaurant, shoulders back, as if marching into battle.

Which there was likely to be. But until then, he'd enjoy watching her hips sway, her glossy hair brush her shoulders, and the way her chin jutted out resolutely. She'd lost a little weight, probably from the flu, but she still looked great.

Too bad he couldn't charge ahead as he had almost five years ago and sweep her off her feet.

He almost laughed as he opened the heavy wooden door. He had as much chance of sweeping Lisa off her feet as he did of flying to the moon.

The noise level was high, the crowd obviously enjoying itself. The hostess found them a table against one wall. Placing chips and salsa in front of them, she waited for their order.

"Marguerita?" Sam asked.

Lisa shook her head. "Too soon after being sick. I'll stick to water."

"I'm driving, one beer," he told the waitress. "We'll order now, too. The lady will have the burrito special and I'll have the chile rellenos."

"What if I've changed tastes in the last couple of years," Lisa asked once the waitress left.

"Did you?"

She shook her head, looking around bemusedly. "It seems strange to be here again." She faced him. "And with you."

Sam didn't know what to make of her statement. He never had been able to understand her. "Strange how?"

She shrugged. "It's not a date, yet it almost feels like it."

"We're going to discuss Joey."

"Right."

"And something else."

Her attention caught, she narrowed her eyes. "What else?"

He stared at her, trying to think of the best way to bring up Margot. It wasn't as if he hadn't had months to think up how to tell her. But the words never came. They still didn't.

"After we eat. Let's enjoy the meal first."

She relaxed and took a chip, loading the hot salsa on it and popping it into her mouth. Tears came into her eyes.

"It's great," she said when she could speak again.

For a while, it was as if time hung suspended, Lisa thought, taking another chip. She and Sam had often come to Rosie's for dinner. The food was good and plentiful. Gazing around, she saw several couples she knew. When she met the eye of a friend, Ellie, she waved, then smiled as her friend's eyes widened when she saw Sam.

"Oops, maybe this wasn't such a great idea after all," Lisa murmured.

"Why?"

"Ellie and Martin Taylor are over there and once she saw you and I were together, they began to talk like crazy. I imagine rumors are circulating even as I speak."

He shrugged. "Can't let what others say guide your life. Especially silly rumors."

"Right, silly rumors."

She thought about the kiss in the truck. Had anyone driving by seen them? Recognized them? That'd certainly fuel rumors. Unfounded ones.

Glancing at Sam, she thought about the discovery she'd made. They'd fought their entire marriage. But they'd loved passionately when making up. Did they have anything left between them to start again?

Or was she just lonely and seeking something that wasn't there?

If there were a chance to recapture what they'd had at one time, did she even want to try? Had they burned their bridges said too many unforgivable things, too many hurtful words?

How did Sam feel about her? Would he be interested? He'd kissed her senseless, then apologized. Why? Why not see if she was interested before slamming the door shut?

Unless he really wasn't interested.

And what else did he want to talk to her about beside Joey?

She reached for her glass, her hand trembling slightly. He wasn't going to tell her he was getting married, too, was he? Had he thought Nick's news worse and told her that first? Now with wanting to have Joey spend more time, was he also looking to get married again?

No, she couldn't believe that. He wouldn't have kissed her if that were the case. No matter what had transpired between them, Lisa knew he was an honorable man. One who'd never, ever cheat on someone he'd made a commitment to.

She didn't know why he had kissed her. But the memory of the kiss stayed in the forefront of her mind all through dinner.

They talked sparingly, enjoying the delicious food. Twice friends stopped by the table. Lisa could tell they were dying of curiosity seeing her with Sam but were too polite to ask any questions. Thank goodness for manners--she had no answers to any questions.

Unable to finish the thick burrito with all the accompaniments, Lisa pushed her plate away when she was full.

"Want some dessert?" Sam asked, finishing up the last of his dish.

"No, thanks. Are you ready to talk?"

She swallowed hard. Maybe they should have talked before dinner. Her meal was now like a lump in her stomach. She hated this.

"Can we hammer out an agreement for our son? Without fighting and yelling and making everyone miserable?" Sam asked. "Jason said he saw no problem with getting joint custody."

Jason Ronald was Sam's attorney. Lisa knew he was a good, solid lawyer. Her own attorney, Todd Bennett, had told her so that afternoon when she'd called him to discuss the matter. Of course, Todd didn't have the file at home on a Saturday, but he knew her, knew the situation. And his advice was to go along with the joint custody. There was nothing to hinder such a judgment, so she might as well not fight.

"What exactly are you looking for?" she asked, carefully rephrasing the question from earlier. She remembered when she'd asked him what he wanted, he'd kissed her!

She hoped he didn't notice the heat she could feel creeping into her cheeks when thinking about that kiss.

"Something more than a week or two every few months. I thought maybe we could alternate weeks."

"Are you up to that? Having a little kid around isn't as easy as it looks," Lisa said, wishing she could find the words to change his mind.

Joey'd be gone for days at a time. She'd miss him and be constantly thinking of him and Sam doing things together. Things they might do as a family if....

"I'm sure I'm up to it. Let's try a week at a time at first."

A three year old would be a piece of cake compared to an infant, Sam thought.

"He's little, he might miss me. Then what will you do?" Lisa said.

"He's fitting in great at the ranch. But if he does miss you,

you can come see him."

"Even if it's every day?"

He raised an eyebrow at that. Then shrugged, "Sure, if that's what he needs."

"I might miss him so much by mid week I'd come out to see him even if he's getting on fine."

Sam studied her for a moment. "That wouldn't be a problem. Somehow I find this is going too easily," he said.

"I talked to Todd this afternoon. He made me see I really don't have much choice. You're Joey's father. There's no reason for him not to spend time with you."

Sam looked away, letting his gaze roam around the crowded restaurant, letting the din wash over him. Wishing he didn't have to go on. That they could end the conversation now and head back. He'd get to see Joey before he went to bed.

"Oh-oh," Lisa said, rising. "I'll be right back." She hurried in the direction of the restrooms.

Sam leaned back in the chair, feeling the reprieve. He'd been a stupid fool and now had to pay the piper.

But he didn't like it.

Heck, he almost laughed, who in Tumbleweed didn't know already? Maybe Lisa.

Or maybe she already knew. It didn't matter he was truly and forever stuck.

Margot had no intention of raising the baby they'd made together and he had no intention of letting his son or daughter go to strangers. Taking responsibility was something his father had hammered into him. There was no question of what was the right thing to do.

There was only the question of how Lisa would take the news.

And why should that matter, he asked himself for the twentieth time. She'd left him two years ago. What he did with his life no longer concerned her.

That kiss had been a mistake of monumental proportions. He couldn't get it out of his mind. Nor the images it invoked the two of them together, all night long.

Lisa came back, looking pale and shaky.

"Sorry about that. I guess it's too soon after being sick," she said, sinking gratefully down in her chair. "I hate to cut this short, but I need to get home."

Sam handled paying the check in short order and they were soon in the truck, heading for the Ballantine's home. Lisa leaned her head back, her eyes closed.

"It was too soon," Sam said.

"It was too much spicy food, but my own fault. I thought I was over being sick. Guess not. I shouldn't have eaten all that salsa. But it sure was good going down."

"Don't push yourself so hard, Lisa. You need to get well before moving."

"I also have to make a living. I've been a week away from work, do you know how much that piles up?"

"Yeah, I do. I run a ranch, too, you know."

Lisa nodded, she hadn't forgotten a single thing about Sam Haller.

Sam walked her to the front door of her parent's home.

"Sorry I got sick," she said, opening the door. The evening couldn't end too soon for her. She'd given in with no fight to his wishes about Joey. And she still couldn't forget that kiss.

"Call me when you're ready to head back to Fort Worth, I'll drive you in."

"My mom can take me."

"Hey, I brought you here, I'll take you back. If you need help moving, give a holler. We've got a lot of trucks on the ranch and willing men who can move you in a day."

"Thanks, Sam."

Amazed at the offer, she wondered why he was being so friendly now?

Of course. He'd gotten his way about Joey. He could afford to be magnanimous.

"Good night, Lisa." He turned and headed back to the truck.

She watched, conscious of a niggling sense of disappointment that he didn't even smile at her, much less kiss her again. Sighing softly, she entered the house. The sound of voices from the kitchen let her know where her parents were, but she didn't want to talk with them or anyone tonight.

Slipping quietly to her room, Lisa tried to make sense of the latest turn of events. She'd have bet money on Sam's not wanting anything to do with her again. And lost, if his offer were sincere.

By the time she'd climbed into bed she'd determined that responsibility had prompted the offer of a ride. He'd brought her to Tumbleweed, leaving her car in Fort Worth, so of course he'd felt responsible for returning her.

She remembered the chores and tasks he and Nick had to do around the ranch before anything else. Their dad had insisted drilling in a sense of responsibility that nothing could shake.

She wished his offer had been prompted by something else.

Tuesday morning, Lisa called Sam to take him up on his offer to drive her into Fort Worth the next day.

"That'll be great, Joey doesn't have a lot of toys here so we'll pick up a few. When will you be moving?"

"I still don't have a place here. Until I find something, I'll have to stay in Fort Worth."

"Wouldn't your parents let you stay there?" Sam asked.

"They probably would, if I asked. Which I'm not going to.

Joey and I need our own place."

The silence let her know Sam's views.

"Anyway, if it's not too much trouble, I'll be ready anytime in the morning."

"We'll pick you up at eight. How are you feeling?"

"I'm back to one hundred percent. Sorry about last Saturday night."

"You said that then. We should have gone someplace that served soup."

"See you tomorrow, Sam."

She didn't want him to continue to see her as someone who was sick. She felt fine. Actually more alive than any time in the last two years.

Promptly at eight the next morning, Lisa opened the door to Joey. He flung himself against her, hugging her tightly. She lifted him and hugged back.

"I've missed you. I swear, Joey, you've grown another foot!"

He laughed, tightening his arms around her neck. "No, I haven't, Mommy, I only have two feet."

She laughed and looked at Sam. His intense gaze had her smile fading as a wave of awareness swept through. He came so close to them she thought he might touch her. But he stopped inches away, looking back and forth between her and Joey, his eyes unreadable.

"Ready to go?" he asked in a low, husky voice.

For a moment Lisa almost swayed toward him. His tone reminded her of dark nights of love.

"Mom and Dad want to see Joey for a minute, if that's okay?"

Her gaze met his, clung. For a moment things swirled around, but she couldn't move. Could only stare into Sam's eyes and feel her heart race.

"I'll wait in the truck," he said at long last.

"Don't be dumb, Sam. Come in."

He doffed his hat and stepped inside the house. Lisa set Joey down just as her father came down the hall. For the next few minutes Joey was the center of attention with his grandparents. Lisa watched as he chatted a mile a minute about all he'd been doing on the ranch, feeling a pang of regret she hadn't been there to see all he'd done.

Better get used to it, girl, she admonished herself. It was the way of the future.

"Looks like you're going to be a full-fledged cowboy in no time," her father told him.

"You must come stay with us soon," her mother said, brushing her hand over his hair as if she couldn't get enough of the little boy.

"Do you have horses?" Joey asked.

Everyone laughed.

"No, but I bake a lot of cookies," Margaret said, not above bribing him.

"We better go," Lisa said, conscious of Sam's silent figure. He didn't evidence any impatience, but this couldn't be easy for him.

"I have something for you to take today," Margaret said, holding out a brown bag to Sam. "It's some of those c-o-o-k-i-e-s I made the other day. For later, if you get hungry."

"I'm sure a certain little boy will love them. After lunch."

Margaret patted Sam on the arm. "And big boys, too. It's good to see you again, Sam."

He smiled and nodded, replacing his hat and looking at Lisa. "Ready now?"

The two hour ride passed swiftly. Joey told his mother about his activities, then she looked to Sam for clarification as her son's explanations sometimes left some crucial fact out.

Wistfully she watched the animation and delight on Joey's face. He'd had a wonderful few days. How would apartment living compare? She was worried she would come up on the short end of that stick. Would Joey grow to hate living with her, yearning to spend all his time with his father on the ranch?

Fort Worth seemed crowded and hectic after the slower pace of Tumbleweed, Lisa thought as they drove through the city traffic. Her street looked tired, closed in.

She took a deep breath. It was only temporary until she found a place in Tumbleweed.

All too soon, she had packed some more of Joey's clothes, and an assortment of games, toys and books. He and Sam were leaving. Leaving her alone in Fort Worth.

Five

By Saturday morning, Lisa was seething with impatience. Today Sam was bringing Joey home. She'd risen early, making sure the apartment was spotless not that it needed any attention. She hadn't been able to sleep well the last three nights, so had whiled away the time getting everything cleaned. Even started packing for the pending move.

She'd also been able to catch up on most of her work for Bill Taylor. It was amazing how much time she had on her hands with Joey gone.

And how desperately she needed consuming tasks to keep her mind from thinking about Sam.

It was almost nine. When would they arrive?

She sat on the sofa and tried to leaf through a magazine, but couldn't concentrate. Glancing at the phone she wondered if Sam would call her to let her know when to expect them or just show up.

He hadn't said anything definite about time. Maybe she should call him. If they weren't coming until afternoon, there was no sense her jumping at every sound as if it might be them.

If he didn't call her, she'd call him.

The phone rang a long time before Nick answered it.

"I'm calling for Sam," Lisa said, surprised to hear him. This was the main phone number for the ranch. Nick had an extension, but rarely used it. He had his own phone.

"He must be doing something. I picked up because it rang so long."

"Do you know when he and Joey are coming to Fort Worth?"

"No." The clipped tone let Lisa know he wasn't thrilled to be talking with her.

"Nick, is everything all right? I mean between you and Sam?"

"It's really not any of your business any more, is it Lisa? You made that clear when you left."

"I couldn't stay," she said.

"Well, there's a difference of opinion on that. If I see Sam this morning, I'll tell him you called." With that he hung up.

Lisa replaced the receiver carefully.

She hadn't imagined his hostility the other afternoon. But why? She had never done anything to him.

Unless it was because of Sam's accusations. False accusations. She and Nick had been tight in high school, but drifted apart long before she'd become involved with Sam. Only he'd never fully believed that.

And her actions during their marriage had done nothing to convince him, she acknowledged ruefully.

Pacing the small apartment, she felt restless and unsettled. Her mother called yesterday afternoon with information about a possible apartment available in Tumbleweed. She planned to drive over tomorrow to see it and then spend the rest of the day with her parents. They wanted to see Joey again.

She wished her sister, Sally, would settle down, get married and give her folks a half dozen grandkids. They loved children and it sure didn't look as if Lisa would be providing any more.

The phone rang.

"Lisa, Nick said you called." Sam's impersonal tone startled her.

"I was curious to know when you and Joey would get here," she said, sitting on the edge of the sofa. Despite the coolness in his voice, she felt almost giddy hearing him.

There was a pause on the other end.

"Late."

"Late? How late? Lunch time?"

"After dinner."

"After dinner? I wanted to see him today, not have you show up just when he's ready for bed!"

"He's not really excited about going back to that apartment. I thought if he was tired out by the time we got there, he'd go right to bed and it'd make the transition easier."

"Oh."

Lisa hated hearing Joey didn't want to come home. Though she couldn't blame him. Had it still been their place in Denver, he might not have minded. But they'd only been two months at this apartment too short a time for a little boy to form attachments.

And she had to admit the excitement of a ranch offered a lot more to a small boy than the quiet apartment building with no yard to speak of and no animals.

"You could stay for a while when you drop him off so he'd know you were still available," she suggested.

"I've already promised a trip to the zoo before we get to your place."

She clutched the phone, her heart sinking. They'd made plans for the day, excluding her. "Joey's never been to the zoo before."

"Yeah, he said that. He's raring to go."

She waited a moment, not wanting to give into the urge, but unable to resist. "I want to go, too."

71

"What?"

"It's a first for him and I want to be there when he sees the lions and monkeys for the first time."

The silence stretched out for a long moment. Lisa wondered what Sam was thinking. Please, don't let him refuse.

"I can see the appeal. I'd have liked to have seen his first steps, been there the first time he talked," Sam said slowly.

Lisa's heart tightened. She'd deprived the man of those milestones with her impatience with things, the lack of trust and understanding.

How much had been real and how much her own inexperience and youth?

"I'm sorry, Sam," she said softly. "You should have seen them, too. But please don't keep me from today for revenge."

"I'm not into revenge, Lisa. We'll pick you up at eleven." He hung up.

"Seems to be a tendency with Hallers," she murmured replacing the receiver.

She vowed to teach Joey to always say goodbye before hanging up a phone.

Her heart rose, they'd be here at eleven! Joey and Sam.

She wasn't sure which one she wanted to see more.

Nick leaned against the counter, watching his brother. He frowned when Sam hung up the phone.

"You're taking her with you now?"

Sam shrugged. "She said it's Joey's first time to the zoo and she wants to be part of it."

"Like you were part of all his other firsts?" Nick asked.

"Leave it alone, bro."

"Seems to me you're close to taking up with her again.

Didn't you learn anything before? Does she know about Margot?"

"Not from me," Sam said, rinsing his coffee cup. "Joey!" he called.

"Are you going to tell her?"

Sam shrugged, met his brother's eyes. "I started to. But, the way things are, it really has nothing to do with her. Now I don't know."

"It has something to do with Joey. In a few weeks he's going to have a half-brother or sister."

"So I'll tell him when the time's right."

"How a reasonably intelligent man can screw up his life so much is beyond me," Nick said. "Jennifer's coming over again tomorrow. Can we discuss the reception then?"

Sam nodded.

He rested a hip against the counter when his brother left and gazed out through the screened door.

Good question, he thought. How had he screwed up his life? When he'd been younger, dealing with his father had been his biggest problem. After his death, Sam thought he'd be free.

Until he'd been caught by a pretty, bright, bubbly armful of sexy woman called Lisa. That ended disastrously.

Next step, get roaring drunk during the lonely holidays and end up sleeping with a substitute for his long-gone wife. And father another baby.

One the mother had no intention of keeping.

What else could a man do, but take his child? He'd missed Joey's firsts, but he wouldn't miss the new child's firsts.

No one said it'd be easy. Most people who knew his plans said he was an idiot for even thinking about it. But he couldn't let his baby be raised by strangers.

And who knew, maybe one day he'd find a woman who'd take him on with two kids.

Or maybe not.

He wasn't anxious to venture forth in the matrimonial stakes again. His track record sucked.

"Joey! Are you ready?" he called, shaking off the regrets and moving forward, the only way he knew how.

When the little boy came skidding into the kitchen, Sam felt his heart swell with love. The kid had Lisa's chin and her way of jutting it forward sometimes. But other than that, he looked like he and Nick had as boys. No question he was a Haller.

"Ready to go to the zoo?" he asked, scooping him up and hugging him gently.

"Yes. We're going to see monkeys and lions!"

"And Mommy. She's going with us."

"Has mommy been to the zoo before?" Joey asked, his expression suddenly serious.

"I don't know."

Amazing after being married two years and hearing about her from Nick when they were all younger, he didn't know that about Lisa.

What else didn't he know about his former wife?

"I'm sure we'll have fun exploring together."

Lisa was standing out front when Sam drew up. She smiled brightly and hurried to the curb, opening the passenger door as soon as he came to a stop in front of the apartment building.

"I thought I'd save you hunting a parking place. Hi, Joey."

She kissed her son on his cheek and slid into the seat, closing the door.

"Thanks for including me," she said to Sam, trying to judge his mood. His face was impassive.

"We're going to the zoo, Mommy!" Joey said excitedly, bouncing in the car seat. "Have you been there before?"

"I sure have, but not for a long time."

"Did you go as a child?" Sam asked, pulling back into traffic.

"Many times. Mom and Dad took Sally and me every summer when we were younger. Did your family go every year?"

"No. I was seventeen the first time I went," Sam said.

Lisa looked away, embarrassed at not knowing.

And embarrassed when she remembered his childhood. She always felt that way when he'd mention the way things had been so different from her own. He never complained, but she knew from her days of dating Nick how hard their father had been on both boys, but especially Sam because he was the oldest. Ben Haller hadn't had time for foolishness, as he called anything frivolous or fun.

Of course, he'd had time for his own pursuits and neglected the ranch more and more as he'd grown older. It'd been a mess when Sam and Nick inherited.

She cleared her throat. "I never told you, but I think what you've done with the ranch has been terrific."

Sam threw her an odd look. "What brought that up?"

Nervously, she traced a design on her jeans. "Just thought I should tell you."

"Why?"

"Does everything have to have a reason?" she said, irritated he couldn't just take the compliment and let it ride.

"Usually."

"Okay, I was thinking about the zoo, then I thought about your father, and then how the ranch was when you first inherited it. I guess I didn't realize back then how much work would be needed to keep it going, much less recover from the neglect."

"And now you do?" he asked, his tone skeptical.

"Maybe not everything, but I sure have a much better appreciation after working with Bill Taylor's place. I see all that needs to be done and remember your doing so much by yourself when we were married."

"So after all this time, and getting insight from a stranger, you suddenly realize I wasn't just trying to avoid spending time with you but had legitimate reasons for the work I was doing?"

"I'm not sure I'd put it that way."

Though it was exactly the way it should be put. But it reminded her how much of the breakup had been her fault. And she hated admitting that.

"How would you put it?" he asked.

Lisa thought a moment, then sighed softly.

"Exactly that way. I'm sorry, Sam. You were working hard and I should have been helping, not adding burdens."

"Water over the dam," he said briefly.

She asked Joey about his visit, listening with half an ear as he talked about horses and cows and steers. She wondered if he knew the difference with cattle yet. If not, it wouldn't be long. His animated expressions were precious. She'd missed him so much.

Better get used to that, she admonished herself. It looked as if there was no help for the change in custody arrangements. She really had no grounds for fighting it.

She kept flicking glances at Sam. He looked bronzed from the sun, fit and trim. His hat rode back on his head and his shoulders filled out a good portion of the wide truck cab. Wishing to hear his voice, she tried to come up with an innocuous topic that wouldn't be controversial, but which would let her hear his deep tones, the soft Texas drawl so appealing.

She'd loved nights they'd spent together in the dark talking, making plans. She remembered listening to him dream about expanding the herd, trying different strains, adding more fields of experimental grains.

He'd respected his wife enough to share his life and dreams with her.

She, instead, had wanted to go dancing, partying and escape the constant workload. A child's view of marriage. She'd been too young to know what to realistically expect. And too young to pull her own weight.

She'd grown up in the last two years.

Had she changed enough to interest Sam?

She looked at him again and felt her heart catch. He was still the sexiest man she'd ever seen.

They were different people from who they'd been when they married, and from when they divorced. He seemed harder, more self-contained.

How much was a cover for the hurt she'd inflicted?

She still felt that strong pull of attraction, even though it was awkward to be around him. The angry words they'd hurled at each other seem to echo whenever she saw him.

Would they one day have a comfortable truce?

How did he feel about her?

The kiss the other night had been fantastic. Surely that showed some interest in more than a truce!

Or was he just reverting to form? She remembered laughing with Nick over some of the wild stunts he and his older brother had pulled around town. And they'd included their fair share of escapades with girls.

Sam's turning into the parking lot for the zoo interrupted her musing.

Joey's exuberance was catching. Lisa felt buoyed up and excited about the outing despite her awkwardness around Sam.

Exploring the different habitats of the animals proved both fun and educational. Sam and Lisa took turn reading aloud the display signs before each enclosure, teaching Joey and learning new facts themselves.

By the end of the afternoon, they were more relaxed and almost chatting comfortably together. Granted the topics of conversation were centered on the zoo or their son, but at least the awkwardness had fled.

It felt surreal, she thought at one point. The two of them had always shared a similar sense of humor, and today they were laughing like old friends. Yet nothing else was the same. They'd been as intimate as anyone could be, and fought like crazy. Now they were acting like polite strangers.

Was that the way it would always be in future?

Poignantly, she wished they'd at least be friends. She hadn't wanted their marriage to turn out as it had. Even now, she wasn't sure exactly how everything evolved. Once started, it had been like a run-away freight train, out of control. Sam deserved better than he'd got.

"Can you carry me?" Joey asked, reaching up his arms to his father.

"Tired?"

"No."

But as soon as Sam picked him up, he laid his head on his shoulder and closed his eyes.

"I bet he's exhausted. He's covered at least twice the ground we have running back and forth like he did," Lisa said, reaching up to pat his back.

She studied Sam holding the boy, feeling a tug at her heart. She imprinted the memory for all time. Who knew when she'd see them like this again? For one bittersweet afternoon, they'd been a complete family.

"Guess we should head for home. Would you like to stay for dinner?" Lisa asked. "I'll fix something quick or we can call for pizza. One of the advantages of living in town, instant pizza delivery."

She said it lightly, instantly hoping Sam wouldn't be reminded of one of her complaints at the end that she could never order pizza because no one delivered so far from town.

"There are lots of advantages of living in a city," he said as they headed for the exit.

"And a lot to living on a ranch."

Were they taking opposite roles in the old debate? How ironic.

Joey was still asleep when Sam carried him into the apartment a half hour later.

"Will he sleep through the night?" he asked.

"I expect so. It's only a couple of hours before he'd normally go to bed, and after all that walking and excitement, I'm sure he's exhausted."

"What about dinner?"

"With all the popcorn and ice cream he ate this afternoon, on top of that whopping burger for lunch, I suspect he'll survive until breakfast. I'll put him down if you like." Lisa took the sleeping child and headed down the short hall.

Sam watched her, then looked around the living room. Quite a difference from the other time he had seen it. It was spotless just as he expected. In the corner were two large cardboard boxes, already half full with books and nick-knacks.

A quiet satisfaction unexpectedly filled him. She was moving closer. He'd get to see her – Joey that is – more frequently.

He turned his hat in his hand, wondering what he was doing. If Joey stayed asleep, there was no need to remain. He could head for home, get something to eat on the way.

But he didn't move, just waited.

"You're staying, aren't you?" she asked a few minutes later, coming into the living room and seeing him standing near the door.

"Guess I will. I haven't had pizza in a long time."

"Me, either. Do you still like everything on it?" she asked, moving to the side table to pull out the phone book.

"Yes."

"Me, too."

In a few minutes she'd placed their order and brought each a glass of red wine from the kitchen. Sam sat on the sofa. Lisa sat on the edge of one of the flanking chairs. A blind man could tell she was nervous.

Interesting, Sam thought, sipping the wine. He'd have rather had a beer. It was as if they were strangers, trying to be polite, with nothing in common to bind them together.

Nothing like the days they'd been dating. His gaze dropped to her mouth, remembering her taste. He took a large swallow of the wine and looked away. Thinking like that could only get him into trouble. Look at what happened when they went to dinner the other night. He'd been unable to keep from touching her, from kissing her.

"So how was it having a three year old around all the time," she asked.

"Challenging. Time consuming. And a lot of fun. I'm going to miss him this week."

"But you'll be able to get lots more done. I didn't realize how much until he was gone these few days."

"The advantages of living in Tumbleweed. If you have a rush project, just call. I'll take him. Find anything yet? I noticed you started packing."

"Mom called with a possibility. I'm going to check it out tomorrow."

What did you talk about to an ex-wife, he wondered. How personal could he get? Did she want to talk about her job or about Joey? Or about the past or the future? Did she want to hear about what he was doing? Or was the severing of legal ties one of many severings? Had all interest waned?

His presence obviously made her nervous. Because Joey had gone to sleep, was she regretting her offer of dinner? He'd eat quickly and leave.

She looked directly at him. "Are you happy with Nick's choice for wife?" she asked.

"I like her."

"That's all?"

"What else? I've only know her a few months and we haven't exactly spent a lot of time together. She and Nick plan to live in his house. They're going to hold the reception in the main house. That's why she was there the other day. They're wanted to discuss the reception."

"Uh, sorry. I guess you didn't get much discussed."

"She and Nick are coming over tomorrow. There's plenty of time. The wedding's not until June, after school is out. Still two months away."

"Big weddings take a lot of planning."

"They've been planning it since Christmas. How long does it take to buy a dress, order some food and reserve the church?"

"There is more involved than that."

"Wasn't with ours." He looked at her sharply. "Did you wish for something different for our wedding?"

She shook her head. "I just wished for something different for our marriage," she said without thinking.

Before he could respond, the pizza arrived.

The next few minutes were busy. He paid the delivery man over Lisa's protests. She brought plates and napkins and offered more wine which he declined. They began to eat and the moment to follow up on her statement passed.

Not that he had a clue what he'd have said.

There were still two pieces of pizza left when Sam reached his limit. Lisa finished eating a few minutes ago.

He tossed his napkin on the plate and looked at her.

"I guess I'll head out."

"I can fix some coffee before you go," she said quickly.

"No need."

"I'd like to."

Coffee meant staying longer. The tension between the two of them had eased somewhat, the day at the zoo had seen to that. But he still didn't know where they stood. Stay or go?

"All right, coffee'd be nice."

She smiled and jumped up to head into the kitchen. Sam gathered the plates and the almost empty cardboard box of pizza and carried them into the small kitchen. He put the dishes in the sink, and the box on the counter.

"Where's your stuff to wrap food in?" he asked, looking around.

"In that drawer," she pointed, grinding fresh coffee. "But you don't have to do anything. You're a guest. Go sit down."

"I don't mind."

He'd rather be doing something than just sit. Especially the way his thought were moving.

He wrapped the pizza and put it away, conscious of Lisa only inches away. She finished grinding the coffee and put it in the filter, starting the coffee maker.

The small kitchen didn't offer much space, he thought, leaning back against the counter and watching her. Her nervousness viably increased.

He almost smiled. At least he wasn't the only one feeling the strain.

The silence stretched out while the machine took its time brewing the fragrant beverage. The aroma filled the room.

"Sam," she said, turning the cups around on the counter

until the handles matched. Moving them a scant millimeter to the left.

"What?"

Darting a quick glance, she returned her gaze to the cups. "The other night, you apologized for kissing me in the car. Is there, was there a reason you shouldn't have?"

He went on alert. This was the last topic he expected her to bring up. "Like what?"

"I don't know conflict of interest or something."

"Because of wanting to spend more time with Joey?"

She nodded, peeking up again, looking away.

Had she thought as much about that blasted kiss as he had? Endlessly replaying every delicious, hot millisecond when she should have been pay attention on something else?

"I didn't think you'd be receptive," he said slowly.

She cleared her throat. "You caught me by surprise. But I wouldn't say I was exactly unreceptive. The thing is, I'm not sure you needed to say you'd never do it again. I mean, you so often hold fast to everything you say and what if you, if *we,* wanted to...just give a quick kiss goodbye or something. As Joey's parents, I mean."

He unfolded his arms, stepping close enough to feel the warmth she generated. When she looked up into his eyes, hers were plain scared.

"So are you suggesting that once in a while strictly as Joey's parents we might want to give each other a quick kiss goodbye?"

She cleared her throat again. "Maybe."

"Goodbye," he said, closing his mouth over hers.

Six

Glorious sensations exploded. Lisa scarcely had a second to take a breath before she was plunged into the maelstrom of desire. Heat flooded, swept through every cell in her body. Her breath left, but she didn't have time to take another, she was too busy savoring the pleasure Sam's embrace brought, relishing the tingling shivers flashing across her skin at his touch.

His mouth was magical. His lips were warm and demanding, and she was delighted to respond.

They'd always been so hot together. So perfect. So magical. She didn't think, didn't remember, only felt the shimmering sorcery of his touch.

Slowly she came back to earth when he eased back from the kiss. Resting his forehead on hers, he stared deep into her eyes.

"You still pack a wallop," he said in that husky voice she remembered so well.

"So do you," she whispered.

Sam stepped away, letting his arms fall to his side.

"I'll take a rain check on the coffee," he said, already turning for the living room.

Before Lisa could gather her wits, he was already at the front door, Stetson in hand.

"Wait!" She dashed into the living room. Stopping at the doorway, she looked at him. "Don't go."

"Lisa, when a man's been through all I've been through, he finally learns some sense. Staying any longer would blow all that sense clear out the window. Call me if Joey needs anything."

She watched in disbelief as he left. Running her tongue over her slightly swollen lips, she could still taste him. Her heart raced, her entire body yearned for his touch. For more than a kiss-- extraordinary as it has been.

It obviously hadn't meant the same to him. She wouldn't have been able to walk away so casually. In fact, Lisa was rather afraid she wouldn't have walked away at all!

The apartment her mother told her about was in an old Victorian home that'd been converted to flats. Leaving Joey with his doting grandparents the next day, Lisa walked over the few blocks separating her parent's home from the Victorian.

The day was balmy, with a hint of high heat threatening. With the cloudless blue sky above her, and the wide lawns and huge old trees lining the sidewalk as she walked over, Lisa knew this was the place to raise her son. The hectic noise and commotion, traffic, billboards, and other trappings of the city were gone. Here was a slower pace of life, friendly neighbors and lots of open space.

The Victorian house had been turned into apartments years ago. Lisa studied the house as she drew closer. It was in good shape, freshly painted, with a huge front yard. If the back was as large Joey'd have lots of room to play. Maybe they'd even let her hang a swing from one of the limbs of that old oak, she thought as she walked up the brick walkway.

A truck pulled in to the sidewalk behind her and Lisa glanced over her shoulder surprised to see Nick Haller.

He climbed out, studied her for a moment, then headed toward the house.

"What are you doing here?" he asked.

"Hello to you, too," she said, determined not to get riled by his hostility.

He stopped beside her.

"Where's Joey?"

"At my folks. I'm here to see about an apartment. The one on the ground floor is available."

He looked at the house and back at her. "Why are you moving back?"

"For a number of reasons, actually. Does it matter?"

"Stay away from Sam."

"What?" That was the last thing Lisa had expected.

"You heard me. You did a number on him before. He's finally gotten over you. And he has enough on his plate right now. Stay away."

"I'm not moving back here to make a play for Sam."

"Aren't you?"

Lisa glared at him. "No, I'm not. I'm moving back to make things easier for Joey. Not that it's any of your concern. And I'm surprised at your attitude toward Sam. He was quick enough to accuse us of cheating behind his back when there was never anything going on. You were mad enough two years ago."

"Yeah, well things change. We could have done more to convince him. At the time, I was torn from not believing he truly believed what he was saying to feeling a bit proud my brother was jealous of me. Stupid reaction."

The anger suddenly left Lisa.

"No more stupid than I was." She glanced at the house and sighed. "I thought he'd fight for me. To show me he really cared. Once started, I couldn't figure out a way to back out and not look like a total idiot."

86

"You are a total idiot," Nick said.

She looked at him again, startled.

"He was crazy for you. You didn't realize when you had it good," Nick said.

"I know."

For the first time she faced it squarely. She'd been the primary cause of their broken marriage.

And she didn't like admitting that even to herself.

"It took him a long time to get over you, Lisa. Don't mess with him again."

"Or?" she challenged.

"Or I'll see you regret it," he said solemnly.

"What's between Sam and me is between the two of us."

"Not any more. There are-- "

"Nick!" Jennifer came out onto the porch. "I saw your truck arrive and wondered what you were doing." She smiled uncertainly at Lisa. "Hi, Lisa. I didn't know he was talking with you."

"We're finished." Lisa turned back to Nick. "I'm all grown up now, Nick. And I can take care of myself and my son."

"Just remember what I said," he said, turning toward Jennifer.

Lisa watched him take the other woman in his arms and kiss her before they both went into the house. Following slowly, she wondered if she wanted to have an apartment in the same place Jennifer did.

After Nick's warning, she wasn't anxious to see a lot of him, and she suspected he was over here quite a lot. Or would be until they married.

Bolstered with the thought it would only be for a couple of months before Jennifer was gone, she continued to the apartment.

The manager showed her the space and answered all her

questions. In less than an hour, Lisa decided to take the spacious apartment.

Despite Nick's unfriendly behavior, she wanted to tell Sam. She'd wait until he called about picking Joey up for another visit, but wondered what his reaction would be.

She found out that evening. Joey was fresh from his bath and ready for bed when the phone rang.

"Hello?" Lisa answered, glad to sit down for a moment. She'd been on the go since early that morning.

"Lisa?"

His voice caused her to catch her breath.

"Hi, Sam."

"I called to see how the apartment hunting went. Did you like the place your mother recommended."

"Yes. Actually, I signed a lease. We move in as soon as we want. It's already vacant."

"Where?"

"That's a funny thing. It's in the building Jennifer lives in."

"Wait until she hears that."

"She might already know. Nick knows I was looking there. He didn't tell you?"

"No."

"Oh. I saw him as I was walking there. Maybe he forgot all about it once he saw Jennifer."

"When are you moving?"

"This week or next. I need to check with Bill to see what the work load's going to be like. He offered to lend a couple of cowboys "

"I told you, I'd send someone. We can do it on Thursday, if that's good for you. Or move the stuff while you're working. Just mark which rooms you want what stuff in."

"You don't have to do that, Sam," she said softly.

"Do you want the help?"

"I'm grateful for the offer. But just because we were married once, doesn't mean I expect you to take care of me now. I can find my own movers."

"Let's not talk about the past, Lisa. I didn't do such a good job of taking care of you and we both know it."

She was shocked. "That's not true. You were super. It was my fault. All of it."

"The anger and jealousy with Nick?" he asked, a trace of amusement in his tone.

"I wasn't jealous of Nick and you had no reason to be. I should have done more to convince you, and maybe stayed away from Nick until you were convinced."

"You don't sound so sure."

"He was a friend. When you and I fought, he always had a friendly ear. That's all it was, Sam. Truly."

"I know. Now. They say hindsight is 20-20."

"I wish I'd done things differently," she said. Being around Sam reminded her of the wonderful hours they spent together when they weren't fighting. It'd been the most special time of her life.

She wanted that special feeling again.

Taking a deep breath, she plunged forward.

"Thank you for offering. I'll take you up on it. I'll check with Bill about Thursday. I'd like to be there if I can."

"Let me know. How's Joey?"

"Tearing around the place. I think you let him run wild in the outdoors. He says the apartment's too small."

She wasn't going to tell Sam how he'd railed against not being at the ranch, how he'd wanted to go there that afternoon instead of his grandparents' place.

"Kids need to be outside," Sam said.

"The new place has a nice yard in both the front and back."

"And he'll be close by. He can come just for the afternoon some days."

"I guess."

It'd be easy to dash to the ranch and back to Tumbleweed in a short time. Nothing like the airplane trips he used to make to see his dad. She held the receiver out to Joey.

"Want to talk to Daddy."

If she wasn't careful, Joey would fall so in love with the ranch, he'd never be happy any place else.

Or like being with his dad so much, he was unhappy being with her.

Of course she understood the latter. She'd felt discontent ever since she'd left Sam.

Was there a way to rectify the situation--to recapture what they'd once had and build upon it?

Could she make her ex-husband fall in love with her all over again?

Or was what they'd had gone forever?

Only one way to find out, she thought. And moving to Tumbleweed would prove the best way to put it to the test.

If she dared.

By Thursday afternoon , Lisa questioned her outrageous plan to try to seduce Sam. She'd been around him all day and never detected the slightest bit of interest beyond getting the job done.

He and four cowboys had shown up at her apartment building, complete with five big pickup trucks. Before mid-morning, her furnishings had been loaded in the trucks and headed for Tumbleweed.

Lisa had only to vacuum and clean the kitchen and she was soon following.

Sam had everything organized when she reached the old

Victorian that'd now be home.

He treated her as if she were some stranger--impersonally friendly, but nothing more.

Even when they finished, he merely tipped his hat and left with the others. They were laughing and discussing a rendezvous at the local country-western bar.

Wistfully, she wished he'd included her in the invitation. Joey was at her mother's.

Sam could have stayed long enough with her to have a beer or two.

Had she read the signs wrong?

Putting away her kitchen utensils, pots and pans, and all the food she'd brought, took most of the remainder of the afternoon.

By ten that evening, the apartment was almost the way she wanted it. Joey was asleep, excited to be so close to his father. He'd talked about going out to the ranch on Saturday. The week had flown by.

Lisa couldn't stand it any longer. She picked up the phone and dialed the main ranch number. If Nick answered, she'd hang up. But if Sam was home

"Haller."

"Hi Sam." She hoped she wasn't making a fool of herself.

"Lisa?"

"I just wanted to call to thank you again for moving all my stuff today."

"You're welcomed."

"With so many men helping, it went fast. I wish you could have moved me from Denver."

"If I'd known you were moving, I might have offered."

For a moment she hesitated. There was so much between them, behind them. Could she ever make this work?

91

"Um, what time do you want me to bring Joey out on Saturday?"

"Bring him early."

She remembered last Saturday when they'd all gone to the zoo. It'd been a special day.

"How about I bring a picnic lunch. We could come around lunch time, I'll stay for the picnic and then leave."

"Want to go riding? We could head for the stream on the southern boundary. It's too cold to swim yet, but Joey could skip stones."

"That'd be great. We'll be there by noon."

Lisa wanted to stay on the phone, continue the tenuous connection with Sam. But she couldn't think of another word to say.

"See you then." Sam severed the connection.

She put down her phone and took a deep breath. That'd been easier than she suspected. Now if only the day itself would prove as easy. But she doubted it. Nothing was easy with Sam Haller.

Sam replaced the receiver and leaned back in the chair. He'd muted the television before he picked up. Now he watched the moving figures with no sound.

Lisa's call had surprised him. As had her suggestion for a picnic. He guessed things would be different with Joey around. He knew Lisa was used to having their son with her and it'd be hard for her to relinquish him every other week. Was this her way of staying around as long as possible?

Or was there another reason?

For a moment he wondered if Nick's comment earlier had any merit? Was Lisa making a play for him?

He doubted it.

But for a moment he let his fantasy take wing--Lisa, back in his life for good. Had they learned enough from their mistakes to avoid them in the future?

Or would the old patterns take hold?

No reason to let them, he thought. He was older and wiser now. Much wiser.

And Lisa, herself, had changed. She was more mature, more practical in her outlook. Maybe....

Maybe pigs could fly, he thought in disgust. It was past time to get on with his life. He flicked the button on the remote and the sound flooded in. Live in the present, not some fantasy world, he told himself.

Saturday dawned as perfect as it gets. The wide Texas sky was a deep blue, without a trace of clouds. The sun shone brilliantly, flooding the air with warmth, yet the heat of the summer was still weeks away.

Sam did his chores in a state of anticipation that grew as the clock moved closer to noon. He tried to tell himself it was for Joey, but he knew he lied. He couldn't wait to see Lisa again.

He'd kept his distance on Thursday, to keep his sanity. After that kiss in her kitchen, he dare not relax his guard for a moment especially around men who worked for him. He'd learned enough about gossip over the last few months to know he'd never consciously do anything to feed the flames again.

The after-moving party at the country-western bar seemed flat with Lisa not there.

He'd stayed the bare minimum he needed to before escaping without causing comment. He'd have left even earlier if he'd known Lisa might call.

Leading the two horses out of the barn, he tied them to the rail fence. He'd saddled his normal mount and the mare Lisa used to like. Would she remember?

"Going for a ride, boss?" Jose asked as he walked up.

"Out to the creek. You need anything?"

"Naw, just coming to check on that gash on Sundown's leg. Vet said to keep it clean and you know how he likes to roll in the dust. That boy of yours coming again?"

"Today. He's the one going with me on the ride. Thought he'd like to play by the water."

"He's a handful, that one. Chip off the old block, huh?" Jose grinned and nodded, heading into the dark barn.

Sam felt the pride fill him with the comment. He loved his son and was proud of him.

The car drove down the long driveway and veered toward the barn when Lisa saw him. He waited by the horses, watching, savoring the anticipation. He could see her behind the wheel. In only moments she was out of the car, releasing a wild bundle of energy who came running toward Sam.

"Daddy! I'm here!"

Joey flung himself into Sam's waiting arms. Standing, Sam smiled over his head right into Lisa's eyes.

"I see you're here. Both of you."

She nodded and reached back into the car to pull out a cloth sack. He watched as the snug jeans pulled tight over her rounded bottom. Swallowing hard, Sam looked away. Lisa had suggested a picnic, nothing more.

"I brought everything we'll need," she said, slamming the door with her hip. She carried two bags.

"We can hitch them behind the saddles."

Sam put Joey on the ground and went to take one sack. His fingers brushed against hers and he felt the warmth of her soft skin. For a moment he hesitated. They'd discussed kissing goodbye, did that include a hello kiss?

She smiled and moved to the mare as if she'd been doing it

every day for the last two years.

Sam spun around and soon had his sack tied firmly behind the saddle. Lisa had also finished the task.

"One more bathroom stop and we'll be ready," she said. "Come on Joey."

"I want to ride with Daddy," Joey said when they returned a few minutes later.

"Sure thing, partner. Let's get Mommy on her horse first, okay?" Sam suggested.

"I think I can mount myself," Lisa said indignantly.

"Check the stirrups."

"Someone else use this saddle recently?"

"Jennifer," Sam said, watching as she easily swung into the saddle. The stirrups were a little long for her, so he moved to adjust them, trying to ignore the warmth of her leg inches from his face. Maybe he should have let her adjust her own stirrups.

"All set," he said, looking up at her.

She smiled at him and he felt his heart kick into overdrive. She had the prettiest smile he'd ever seen.

"Thank you, Sam."

"Let's go, Daddy!"

In only a minute Sam and Joey were mounted and ready to ride. They left at a walk, Lisa looking around as if trying to see changes since she left. Joey kept up a running commentary of things he wanted to eat for lunch giving Sam a full rundown of everything Lisa had fixed.

"No surprises for lunch," Lisa said. She laughed at Joey's enthusiasm.

"Sounds great. I can't wait to eat," Sam said.

"Me, too," Joey chimed in.

They crested the small rise that hid the creek from the house and trailed down the slope to the water's edge. Cottonwoods grew along the banks, affording shade. The grass was still green from the spring rain.

Dismounting, they soon had the picnic blanket spread and the food out. Joey took a drumstick and began to eat, beaming at his parents.

Lisa felt his happiness herself. Looking at Sam, she met his gaze. Once again she felt as if they were silently communicating both knowing what the other thought. Love for their son was something easily shared.

"This is fun," Joey said.

"Yes it is," Lisa quickly agreed, smiling at Sam.

He stretched out on his side, eating the chicken. Lisa had always had a way with southern fried chicken. He remembered what a great cook she'd always been. Pete's chuck couldn't compare.

Not that her cooking was the only thing he missed when she'd left.

"You're quiet," she said.

"Thinking."

"Not on a picnic. This is a time for having fun. If you want to think dark thoughts, do it on your own time."

He raised an eyebrow. "Dark thoughts?"

"You were frowning."

"Couldn't have been, I was thinking how good the food is and what a great cook you are."

Color stained her cheeks. "Thank you."

For a moment, she looked flustered. Sam liked that look.

"I didn't know you thought I was a good cook."

"Great," he corrected. Taking another piece of chicken, he looked at her. "Didn't I mention it before?"

She shrugged. "I don't remember it if you did."

"Probably too busy yelling."

Startled she stared at him, then burst out laughing. "I guess we're not going to pussyfoot around the past."

"No need. We both know what was there. Nothing's changed, has it, Lisa?"

She hesitated a moment.

"I don't know, Sam. I think some things have changed. I have for one."

He sat up and reached for one of the soft drinks she'd brought, popping the top. He looked at it for a moment, then raised it up to drink. Stalling. He knew it. But he didn't have an answer to her comment.

"Can I go play in the water?" Joey asked. "I'm finished."

"It's too cold to play in the water today, son." Sam said, glad for the reprieve. "We can skip stones, though."

"What's that?"

"Come on and I'll show you."

He looked at Lisa and she smiled again. She was doing that a lot today.

"I'll watch you from here. When you get back, there's chocolate cake."

"My favorite."

She nodded.

He headed to the water's edge with Joey.

Everything she'd brought was a favorite. Had she done it deliberately? Or was it coincidence? Most of the fare was usual for picnics.

He found some flat pebbles and showed Joey how to skip them across the surface of the wide, slow-moving creek. The little boy tried time and again, but could only make a big splash with his stones.

Lisa called encouragements.

"You come, Mommy," Joey called back. "You come skip rocks."

Lisa joined them on the edge, searching for the perfect

stone. She skipped it four times and turned to Sam, her eyes sparkling.

"Show off," he said, throwing another one. This one skipped six times.

"Me a show off," she muttered, hunting again for another stone. Before long, they were vying with each other on who could skip the most times.

Lisa laughed and sent another pebble skimming across the top of the water, skipping seven times.

"Wow, that's the most I've ever done," she exclaimed, clapping Joey's hand in a high five.

"Not bad for a girl," Sam said. He grinned at her mock anger and sent a stone flying only to have it plop and sink without a single skip.

Her laughter rang out. It did funny things to his heart. He had missed the laughter. her passion and zest for life. She threw herself into everything wholeheartedly.

Including that kiss the other night.

He had to stop thinking about that kiss.

Joey threw a rock, making a big splash. He clapped his hands. "This is fun."

"The whole day is fun," Lisa agreed, smiling directly into Sam's eyes.

He wasn't blind. She was making a play for him. There was no question about it. And he wasn't one to question why.

Leaning over, stopping a scant inch from her mouth, he gazed into her eyes. "Winner gets a kiss?" he said in a low voice.

"Do I win with seven skips?" she asked, flirtatiously, her own gaze dropping to his mouth.

He almost groaned with the intensity of feelings that surged. Closing the distance, his mouth covered hers. Sam savored the taste of her, the heat that enveloped them. For a moment, everything else faded, the water, Joey, the remnants of the picnic. There was only Lisa and him, alone in a world of their own.

"Mommy, I throwed a rock." Joey pressed against Lisa's leg, trying to separate his parents.

Breaking the kiss, Sam's gaze never left hers as he pulled back. "Good for you, Joey."

She licked her lips and turned to face her son. Sam turned away, wishing for a split second that Joey had not come with them. If he and Lisa had been alone....

What was he thinking of? They wouldn't have been together at all today without Joey. And the last thing she wanted was a roll in the hay with her ex-husband no matter how much he might want that!

He was playing with fire. They were on a family outing, nothing more. And once they finished the picnic, they'd head for home--their separate homes.

"It's hard to tell who was the clear cut winner, wouldn't you say," Lisa said. "Want to try best two out of three?"

He swung around. What was she up to?

Seven

Lisa almost laughed at the expression on Sam's face. Normally he never let anyone know what he was thinking. But she knew he was puzzled by her attitude. Good, time to shake the man up.

"What are you playing at?" he asked.

"I'm not playing. I'm deadly serious," she said solemnly.

"About?" He raised an eyebrow again.

"About you and me," she said in a rush.

"There is no you and me."

"There could be."

"I don't think so. We tried it once and got burned."

"So that means you don't want to try again?"

"Got it in one."

"What if I do?'

"Why?"

She looked away, watching Joey's attempts at skipping rocks.

"Maybe I want to give Joey a family. The way it should have been, two parents."

"Most families have two parents who love each other."

Love. Lisa felt the familiar clutch in her heart.

Did she love Sam? She once thought she did. But had it only been illusion? Sex?

"What's love," she asked softly.

"Something neither of us had," he scoffed. Turning he headed for the picnic blanket. "You're kidding yourself and trying to kid me if you think we can make a go of it again."

"We could if we tried," she said, turning to follow him with her eyes.

Sam sat on the blanket and opened the plastic container with the cake. It had tilted and one side was squashed against the container.

"I'm not going down that road again, Lisa. Did you bring a knife?"

She frowned and headed for the blanket. "Yes. I wrapped it so it wouldn't poke anything. Why not?"

"Why not what?"

"Sam! Why not try again."

He looked up, putting down the knife and the cake.

"I could list a whole bunch of reasons starting with I don't want to. Is that what you want, a list of reasons, or will that one do."

"I made a mistake."

"I've made a few."

"I want to make it right."

"It can't be made right."

"Okay, then let's start over. Hi. I'm Lisa Haller."

He shook his head. "Lisa Haller? That's starting over? That's coming with the past."

"So," she almost shouted, "I do have a past. One I'm trying to change."

"You can't change the past, Lisa. No one can." He tossed the knife down and rose to his feet. "I can't change what's happened and neither can you."

"Then maybe we can start over. Why won't you even talk about it?"

"There's nothing to talk about. The answer is no."

She watched him stride away with a growing sense of futility. He wouldn't even discuss the possibility.

What had all those kisses been about?

She rose, torn with wanting to follow him and make him talk and her need to stay with Joey. The creek was too enticing for a three-year-old to be left alone.

Darn, she thought, as she headed back to the bank, the picnic wasn't going like she'd hoped.

"Where's Daddy going?" Joey asked, looking after Sam.

"He'll be back soon. Want to skip more rocks?"

"Can we go wading?"

"No. The water's too cold. Come summer, it'll be nice and warm."

She smiled remembering a summer's afternoon when she and Sam had gone wading and ended up soaked and laughing. Not all her memories of living on the ranch were bad. As she let herself, she remembered a lot of happy times. Why hadn't she remembered those when she got so angry with him?

Lack of balance and maturity, she admitted ruefully. She'd wanted everything her way and nothing in life goes perfectly for anyone.

Sadly, she acknowledged that maybe she couldn't make Sam change his mind.

Again, it was what she wanted but she knew now that a person didn't always get their own way in everything. The last couple of weeks had shown her they could at least be cordial together.

Maybe that was the best she was going to get.

"But I'm not giving up just yet, you stubborn man," she murmured softly, looking after him.

"What?" Joey looked up from the pile of rocks he was stacking.

"Nothing, sweetie. What are you building?"

"A mountain."

"And a fine one it is."

She smiled, happy to see her little boy so delighted with the simple entertainment. It sure beat playgrounds and small apartments.

Sam walked quickly along the creek's edge for a long time trying to out walk his thoughts, distant himself from temptation in the form of Lisa. He clenched his fists against the yearning to take what she was offering and hold on with both hands.

But once burned, twice shy. He'd had a hard time getting over Lisa.

He laughed mirthlessly. Who was he trying to kid? Was he over her? Or would he ever be?

Even when dating Margot, he'd constantly compared the two. Which had been a disservice to Margot. She was a nice woman. She simply wasn't Lisa.

But he suspected he didn't have what it took to make a good husband. He'd blown it the only time he'd tried. And the fallout was too devastating to risk again. They had their son to consider, as well. He dare not risk repeating what happened when Joey was an infant. A baby wouldn't remember his parents fighting. A young boy would.

Sam knew that. He remembered his parents fighting before his mother left.

Did that also color his view?

He stopped and turned toward the creek, watching the water splash and flow to the right, heading for the Brazos. His thoughts were a jumble but foremost was the kernel of happiness that Lisa even said she'd like again.

Granted making a family for Joey wasn't the most ringing

endorsement for an enduring marriage but at least she was talking to him again.

And responding to his kisses.

He clenched his fists again. He had to stop kissing her. She was like an addiction--one taste wasn't enough. He wanted more, yearned for more.

But he was rational enough to know that way lay danger. If one kiss weren't enough, and he wasn't strong enough to resist, one kiss would lead to two and three and then more than kissing.

He reset his hat on his head and turned to walk back downstream. Hiding away helped nothing. He'd see the picnic through, then stay as far away from Lisa as possible.

When he reached the two sitting on the bank, racing sticks in the water like boats, he paused for a moment. The temptation to tell her all about Margot was strong. What if she knew about it and it didn't matter?

He shook his head. On the other hand, what if she didn't?

One word and Lisa would be off like a shot. If she pursued that fanciful notion of getting back together, he'd tell her.

He'd have to tell her sooner or later. When he told Joey. But for now, he'd opt for later.

"America's Cup?" he asked.

"We're racing boats, Daddy," Joey said, grinning happily.

Sam didn't look at Lisa as he hunkered down beside their son. "I can see that. Who's winning."

"We both are," Joey said.

Sam wished everything was that easily viewed.

Lisa rose and dusted off the seat of her jeans.

"I'm going to head back," she said. "I'll leave the horse at the ranch. You two stay. Joey's having fun."

Sam rose. "You don't have to leave."

"There's no real reason for me to stay, is there?" she asked, not meeting his eyes.

Sam wanted to erase the look of disappointment from her expression. But nothing he could say would change things.

"We'll ride back with you."

"No, I'll be fine. I know the way. I recognized the landmarks on the ride here. I might call during the week to talk to Joey if that's okay."

"Of course. Thanks for the lunch, it was delicious."

She nodded and bent to kiss Joey. Then, still without looking at Sam, she headed for her horse. Tightening the cinch, she swung up into the saddle and turned toward the ranch.

Lisa returned home feeling totally discouraged. The picnic hadn't lived up to her expectations. She didn't know what she could have done differently. She parked on the street and saw Jennifer sitting on the porch in one of the rattan rockers as she walked up the flagstone walkway.

"Hi neighbor," Jennifer called gaily, waving. "Want to visit a while? Nick's coming to get me around four and I'm taking time to just veg out. Kids get really rambunctious in the springtime, as I'm finding out."

Lisa smiled politely and debated. "I don't have any other plans," she said, deciding to get to know the woman a bit better. "Oops, that sounded ungracious."

"No it didn't. If you had other plans I wouldn't expect you to cancel just to sit on the porch."

Pulling one of the other rockers across the wooden porch, Lisa sat beside Jennifer, and gazed out over the wide expanse of front lawn. The huge oak trees shaded a portion, including the porch. It was peaceful.

She sighed softly.

"Problems?" Jennifer asked gently.

"Not really. Or at least nothing new. Tell me how you met Nick."

"Ouch. Actually, that's rather embarrassing. He picked me up at a country-western bar. I keep trying to come up with a romantic tale to tell the children. I'm not sure I'd want a daughter of mine picked up in a bar."

Lisa smiled. "Sounds like Nick, however. What's surprising is that he's getting married. He, er, had a rather wild reputation."

"I know all about it," Jennifer said, then grinned. "And those days are behind him if he knows what's good for him. He only gets to be wild with me."

"So you'll be moving to the ranch when you marry?"

Jennifer nodded, rocking back and forth, her expression dreamy. "Yes. I can hardly wait."

"It's not as convenient as living in town."

"I know that. And in winter if we get any snow, it's going to be a bear to get to school. But it'll be worth it." Jennifer looked at Lisa for a moment. "Didn't you like living there?"

Wistfully, Lisa remembered the delight she'd experienced when she'd first moved into the big family home. It'd been such a thrill. And being with Sam had been exciting, a time charged with passion and intensity. But the sheen had quickly dulled. She'd wanted more, and in retrospect knew she'd been after fools gold.

"Yes, I liked it when I lived there."

"It's nice Joey'll have a chance to spend a lot of his growing up on the ranch. Especially if he decides to take it up."

Lisa looked at her in surprise. "Why wouldn't he?"

Jennifer shrugged. "I don't know. If he wanted to be a doctor or something, wouldn't you want him to pursue that career?"

"Oh, I see. Yes, I would."

Jennifer nodded. "Which makes you a better parent than Nick's father."

"Well, that wouldn't take much. He had a terrible reputation in town."

"So I've heard. And justifiably so, from what Nick says. At least he got away for a while. Sam never did."

Lisa looked at her in surprise. "Did Sam want to?"

Jennifer hesitated, then slowly nodded her head. "I thought you knew. He wanted to be a vet. But his father wouldn't even hear of it. He wanted Sam to run the ranch and that was that."

"I can't see Sam kowtowing to anyone even his father."

"Ah, but psychological manipulation isn't hard if someone starts when a person's a child. I know. My parents were terribly over-protective of me. To them I was in danger if I lived a normal life. I didn't even question their views until I was an adult. It was hard to walk away, to move from Virginia to Texas and start out on my own. Sam had twenty years of his father telling him the ranch was his responsibility, that he had an obligation to run it, to build it for future generations."

Lisa shifted uncomfortably on the chair. "I never heard him talk about that."

Was it true? Had Sam really wanted to do something besides run that ranch? He'd never said a word to her during their marriage about wanting to be a vet. He'd talked about increasing the herd, the repairs needed on the buildings, buying new equipment. What they'd do when they had money enough to travel.

Jennifer shrugged. "Sorry if I was letting repeating something that I shouldn't have. I know you're not connected with the Hallers any more, except as Joey's mother. I guess I thought you knew."

"Nick told you?"

Jennifer nodded.

Lisa smiled brightly and stood. "At least you and Nick will start off with communications open between you. That's got to be good. I've got to go."

The reminder she was not connected with the Hallers hurt. Especially when she saw Jennifer had a closer connection than she'd had when she had been connected.

"I did it again, didn't I?" Jennifer said, a stricken look on her face.

"What?"

"Put my foot in it. It's just I'm so much into telling everything so there are no secrets that can harm, I get carried away. Not everyone wants to know the truth, do they?"

"I do. And I'm learning quite a few truths I should have known before. Nick doesn't want me around Sam, did you know?"

Jennifer nodded slowly.

Lisa crossed her arms over her chest.

"Nick and I used to date in high school. I thought he was my friend."

"He was. But your leaving hit Sam hard. I think that was the first time Nick realized his brother was human and not some superman."

"It wasn't easy leaving," Lisa said.

"Then why did you?"

"It was harder to stay. At least I thought so at the time."

"But not now?" Jennifer asked.

Lisa shook her head. "I don't know. When I see Sam... "

Jennifer waited, but Lisa wasn't up to sharing more with this woman she hardly knew.

She smiled politely and shook her head.

"I've got to go. See you."

She spun around and quickly went into the house. Closing the door to her apartment behind her, she leaned against it, feeling as if she'd run a mile.

Her thoughts were jumbled visions of Sam--laughing, yelling, kissing her. The newly discovered knowledge he'd wanted something she'd never known about. A poignant sadness enveloped her.

She hadn't been enough. She knew that now. The marriage ended because she hadn't been enough woman to live with Sam Haller.

And now he wasn't interested anymore.

Lisa spent Monday at the Taylor ranch, needing to fully occupy herself to keep from dwelling on Sam. And Joey. She really missed her little boy.

Was that what Sam felt when Joey was with her?

Her hours on the ranch were full, but the drive there and back left too much time to think.

It was a balm to her ego to find Bill Taylor happy to see her. He discussed the various aspects of the paperwork that needed to be filled out, the accounts to be brought up to date.

Then he asked her to join him in a ride around the property. Lisa had gone with him twice before to survey the newly inherited land. From her two years on Sam's place, she'd picked up quite a bit of knowledge of a working ranch. Knowledge she gladly shared with Bill.

When they reached one field, they stopped and looked at the cattle grazing in the high grass. The winter had been mild with plenty of rain. The spring grass was belly high to the cattle and they made the most of the grazing.

"You should sell some of the older steers and get some new stock," Lisa said, studying the cattle.

"You're right. There's another stock show down in Houston next week. Would you be able to go? I can't go, I have another commitment I can't get out of. But I know exactly what I want to bid on. I've studied the catalog and talked with some other ranchers in the Cattleman's Association. You can bid on them for me."

"Sure, when is it?"

"Tuesday, Wednesday and Thursday. I really appreciate it, Lisa. Will Joey be a problem?"

"No, I'm sure my Mom would love to watch him. Spoil him rotten, I'm sure."

"I've decided to cross breed one part of the herd to see how it does, while keeping the other part pretty much as my uncle started. A couple of new bulls are key."

They continued their survey of the ranch. Lisa made all the right comments, but couldn't help comparing today's ride to the one she'd had on Saturday.

She wished Sam shown her what he'd done while she'd been gone. Talked with her about plans he'd made.

Confided in her about his hopes and dreams.

Sighing softly, she counted the minutes until she could get back in the car and head for home. She'd call the Haller ranch that evening. To talk to Joey.

And to Sam.

Even if he didn't want to see her, she could hear his voice.

It was too bad, she thought, as she drove home from the Taylor ranch, that the stock auction hadn't been week after next, then Joey would be at the ranch and Lisa wouldn't have to miss even more time with her son. But it was her week to have him and now she'd miss three days with him.

It couldn't be helped. She liked her job and appreciated the chance Bill gave her. A more experienced rancher wouldn't want to put up with her own lack of experience. He and she were learning together.

It was after seven by the time she reached home. Tossing

her stack of papers on the sofa, she pulled out her phone.

"Haller," Sam's strong voice answered.

"Hi. It's me, Lisa. Is Joey still up?"

"Sure." Without another word, he called Joey.

Lisa waited impatiently. It wouldn't have hurt Sam to talk to her while she waited for Joey.

"Hi Mommy, I ate all my green beans at dinner. Pete says they make strong cowboys."

She laughed softly. "That they do. Good for you. What did you and Daddy do today?"

Listening to his recount of the day made her miss him even more. How could she wait until Saturday to see him again?

When he was winding down, she said, "Let me talk to Daddy, okay?"

"She wants you," Joey said loudly.

"Yeah?" Sam said a second later.

"Would it be all right if I came by tomorrow afternoon for a little while. I miss him."

"I'm going into town tomorrow. Want me to bring him by for a couple of hours?"

"That'd be great. What time?"

"I need to stop by the bank, no set time. When's good for you?"

"Afternoon would let me get some work done in the morning."

"We'll come around three."

"Thanks, Sam."

He didn't hang up like she expected. Taking a hopeful breath, she asked, "What did you two do besides count all the cows?"

"Guess it seems like that to Joey. We just ran a tally of one section. Yesterday we stayed around the house. Jennifer came by and we discussed their wedding plans. She and Joey hit it off.

Comes from her being a teacher, I guess, knowing how to deal with kids."

"She and I talked some on Saturday."

"Oh?"

"She was on the porch when I got home. There are these really comfortable rockers which just cry out to sit in them and rock away any cares. I sat out there yesterday. Today I went to the Taylor Ranch to get another stack of work. I'm constantly amazed at the paperwork connected with a ranch."

"At least computers have made things much easier."

"Ummm. Jennifer told me something surprising."

"What?"

"That you wanted to be a veterinarian."

"Old news."

"I didn't know."

He was silent.

Lisa rushed into speech, "So it made me wonder what else about you I didn't know."

"Funny, I was thinking that about you when we went to the zoo. Joey asked if you liked to go and I didn't know if you'd ever been."

"Now you know I've been. Why don't you go study to be a vet when your dad died?"

"Too many responsibilities."

"Cop out, Sam. Nick could run the ranch. You could go now."

"I'm too old."

"You're thirty-two. You'd be a bit older than some of the other students, but not by much."

"It takes years, Lisa. I can't just go and presto become a vet."

"I think you should pursue it."

"I'll keep your recommendation in mind," he said sardonically.

She felt the old anger flare, but clamped down on it. She recognized a defense mechanisms now when she saw one.

"All I'm saying is you could do it if you really wanted. Maybe you should stop listening to your father and listen to yourself."

"Advice from an expert?"

"At least I'm trying to learn from mistakes and change things. What are you doing?"

"Living the life I was meant to, I guess. We'll see you tomorrow around three."

"Goodbye," she said quickly and hung up. At least she had that satisfaction.

Promptly at three the next afternoon, the familiar pickup truck pulled into the curb in front of the old Victorian. Lisa sat on the porch in one of the rockers. That was fast becoming her favorite pastime.

Sam got out, helping Joey. The small boy ran across the yard up to the porch. Sam followed more slowly. Reluctantly, if her guess was right.

"I'll be back around five."

"Want to stay for supper?" she asked, hugging her son.

"No."

She looked up at that. "Why not? My cooking's just as good as Pete's."

He nodded. "Better. But you're dangerous to be around."

Lisa felt the warm glow. Slowly standing, she smiled. He found her dangerous, huh? How promising.

"Spaghetti and meatballs and nothing more dangerous, I promise."

He stepped closer, ruffling Joey's hair, gazing down into Lisa's eyes. "Nothing more?"

"Unless you want something more? Garlic bread?"

The smoldering look in his eyes let her know what he was thinking about and it wasn't garlic bread.

"You'll behave yourself?"

Widening her eyes, she nodded. "Always."

He muttered something and turned away. "Okay, supper."

A thought struck. "Sam?" she called.

"What?" He turned on the walkway and looked at her.

"Would you like to have Joey again next week? Then I could have him two weeks in a row following that? I have to go out of town next week. Mom would watch him I'm sure, but I bet he'd like the ranch better."

"Where are you going?"

"To a stock auction in Houston."

"With Taylor?"

"For Bill. He can't go."

Sam was silent a long moment. Then he shook his head.

"I can't watch Joey, I'm going to the same show. Want to drive to Houston together?"

Eight

This was not going to rank up there with the most brilliant thing she'd ever done, Lisa thought as she gazed out of the truck window conscious of Sam sitting a few inches to her left.

What she should have done the minute she heard Sam was going to Houston was call Bill and say she couldn't attend the livestock show.

Or at the very least turned down Sam's offer and insist she drive herself.

But no, she had to agree to Sam's suggestion that she ride down with him. And stay in the same hotel.

Did that mean meals together as well?

She cleared her throat. "I appreciate the ride, but don't want you to feel you have to chauffeur me around Houston. I can get a cab from the hotel to the stockyard."

He glanced at her. "If you like. Seems dumb when I'll be going myself."

"Oh, well, if we happen to be going at the same time, then I guess it does make sense to go together."

Did she imagine the hint of smile? She wasn't sure and she didn't plan to stare at him long enough to find out.

She swiveled her head and gazed determinedly out the side window.

A faint hint of aftershave wafted on the air. She closed her eyes as memories assailed. Behind her lids she could envision the nights they'd spent together, tangled together, tired after working, and making love into the wee hours.

She opened her eyes, unable to bear the poignant reminders of what they'd once had.

"Do you get to Houston often?" she asked, trying for innocuous conversation.

"No."

She glanced at him. He looked totally at ease. His hat was pushed back a bit and she could see the faint line where it rode when down on his forehead. She longed to trace a fingertip over the indentation. Clenching her hands into fists, she quelled the desire. That would only compound her own foolishness.

She deliberately relaxed her hands. She should be using this opportunity to explore their relationship, see what possibilities might present themselves, not act like a nervous teenager on a first date.

They were only a half hour from home, with hours to go before they reached Houston. She'd never have a better time to spend alone with Sam.

"Tell me about Denver," Sam said as the silence stretched out.

"Not much to tell."

"Why did you go there?"

"Job opportunity."

"And Dallas or Houston wouldn't have had them?"

"I was trying to run away," she said, angry to have to put it into words. And embarrassed.

"I was mad at you and Nick, but you didn't need to run so far," Sam said.

"I'll admit I overreacted, okay? I should have just gone home. Or to Austin. Somewhere closer than Denver. But at the time, I was so angry I wanted to put as much distance between us as possible."

"Maine would have done that," he murmured.

She laughed softly. "Not that much distance. I needed to stay in the west. Though working in an insurance office is nothing like a hardware store or a ranch. And I wasn't that crazy about big city living."

"Yet you were going to live in Fort Worth."

"It's closer to Tumbleweed. But it doesn't matter now, does it?"

"No."

That sounded final. She flicked him a glance. "You could have come to Denver to check out where Joey was living."

His eyes met hers for a second, then he turned back to the road. "No, I could not have. I expected Nick to tell me."

She sighed. "Why can't you let it go?"

His hands tightened on the wheel. "It doesn't matter now."

"It seems to, you're still harping on it."

"Harping? I mentioned it, that's all."

"Nick was my friend moreover someone who seemed to understand me a lot better than you did."

"That's Nick--understanding."

"You have no need to be jealous of Nick, Sam. You're twice the man he is."

"I'm not jealous."

"Sorry, my mistake."

They drove for several moments before he spoke again. "Maybe a little."

"What?"

"I didn't like your turning to him when we had a fight. I wanted you to come to me."

"We should have taken a course in communications 101. I've had time to think a lot about what I had and threw away."

"Threw away?"

"You made me so angry, I just took off. I truly thought you'd come after me. Even after that last night, when you thought I'd been with Nick. I thought once you cooled down you'd see how dumb that was and come after me and Joey. You surprised me by not following. And by agreeing to the divorce."

"Heck, Lisa, you told me plain out you never wanted to see me again. I can't read minds. I can only go on what you say. Plus, I truly believed you and Nick had something going and would be getting married once the divorce was final."

"I know that now. I wish I'd know it then."

"I thought I made it plain."

"Only to someone listening."

"You'd have to be deaf not to have heard," he said wryly.

She laughed again. "You do have a, er, carrying voice."

It had not been funny at the time. She'd been furious.

"I yelled as loud as I could, but you yelled right back."

"You know what was totally amazing about that night? That Joey slept through it all," she said.

"Yeah. So tell me about Joey in Denver."

For the next hour or so Lisa regaled Sam with tales of Joey growing in their small apartment. She left out the nights he was sick and she was so scared for their baby, telling him instead of milestones, like walking and talking. And of funny incidents, like his dumping the full bottle of cooking oil all over the kitchen floor then scooting around in the slippery substance. Of his sticking his tongue out at a friendly man at the bank. Of his first attempts at some words and the odd combination of syllables he'd come out with.

By the time they reached Houston, Lisa was feeling hopeful that things were smoothing out between her and Sam.

They parked the truck, each carrying their own small overnight case into the hotel near the stockyards.

"I need a hat," Lisa murmured as they stood in the short line for registration. Glancing around the huge lobby, she noticed dozens of small groups of ranchers and stock men talking and laughing. Every man, woman and child in the place seemed to be wearing a western hat.

"So we'll check out the shops. I bet you'll find one in the first one we go in."

She started to tell him she'd manage on her own, but stopped.

How would they get closer if she was set on being totally independent?

"Thanks, I'd like that."

They were next. When waved to the counter, Lisa stepped aside and looked at Sam. "You go on. I'll wait for the next one."

He looked at her for a moment, then nodded and moved to the registration desk. In less than a minute, another position opened and Lisa when to register.

"Lisa Haller," she told the clerk.

He pulled up her information on the computer, took her credit card and in a short time handed her a folded card with her room key. "You are in 2020, adjacent to Mr. Haller."

She hesitated. "Adjacent to Mr. Haller?" she asked. Had Sam requested they have adjacent rooms.

"Yes, ma'am. It's an adjoining room."

She looked at the key holder for a moment, then picked it up. "Thank you."

Turning, she saw Sam was already talking with some men he knew. She watched him warily as she headed for the elevators. Had he asked for adjoining rooms? Was he planning on using this trip to see what might develop away from home and responsibilities and other people's prying eyes?

Or was it merely coincidence?

Unlikely. Coincidences like that didn't happen.

She slipped inside when the elevator doors slid open. Punching the button for her floor she leaned against the side, out of sight of Sam. Breathing a sigh of relief when the doors slid closed, she tried to decide if she was happy about the arrangement or not.

Unpacking took about three minutes. Three shirts, clean underwear and another set of jeans didn't take long. She was here to work and packed light. Brushing her hair in the bathroom, Lisa splashed water on her face and considered what to do next.

Her phone rang.

It was Sam.

"I ran into some friends. We're going out to dinner in a little while, want to come?"

So much for her idea of a big seduction scene.

"No, thanks."

"Suit yourself. I'll be ready to leave for the auction around seven in the morning. That too early?"

"No, I'll be ready."

"See you then." Sam hung up.

"So much for doing things together," she said aloud.

Well, she'd initially thought she'd be on her own in Houston. She was capable of entertaining herself.

But for a moment, she felt disappointment. Had she misread the signs? Wasn't Sam interested any longer?

Promptly at seven the next morning, her phone rang. Lisa answered it.

"Ready? I'll meet you in the lobby," Sam said.

"Why didn't you just knock on the door," she asked.

"What door?"

"The adjoining one between your room and mine."

The silence was surprising.

"You're in the adjoining room?"

"You didn't know?"

"No."

She walked to the door and opened hers. Knocking lightly on the other she didn't have to wait long before he opened his. She hung up.

"I didn't know you asked for adjoining rooms," he said, following suit.

"I didn't, I assumed you did."

His eyes narrowed. "Why?"

Heat washed through her, flooding her cheeks. "I don't know I just thought you'd asked for adjacent rooms."

"I didn't."

"Oh."

Flustered, she turned and picked up the small backpack that had all her auction information. "I'm ready."

He stepped through to her room and headed out the door. Lisa followed and made sure it was closed.

As they waited for the elevator, Sam studied at her. "You could have mentioned it yesterday when I called."

"I would have if I hadn't thought you already knew."

"Interesting reaction I'd have thought you'd have asked for different rooms at the least."

She shrugged and watched the elevator doors.

"I didn't think you'd suddenly attack. You're the one who said he'd never kiss me again."

"And you said it would be all right to exchange goodbye kisses," he began just as the elevator reached their floor. "Maybe you want something more than goodbye kisses."

Four interested sets of eyes moved from Sam to Lisa as they heard the last comment.

She glared at him. "No, I do not!"

Head high, she stepped into the elevator and turned to face the front, knowing her cheeks had to be scarlet.

Blast the man, he looked as if he were enjoying himself. He nodded to the other occupants and stepped inside beside her.

"We need to get you that hat, too, sugar," he said in a broad Texas drawl.

"I can get my own hat," she hissed.

"Buying a hat won't break the bank," he continued, obviously enjoying her discomfort. "Consider it a return favor."

She glared at him. Then looked at the other occupants. "It's not what you think," she said.

No one met her eye.

She knocked his arm. "Tell them."

He looked at her, amusement dancing in his eyes. "Honey, I told you before, I can't read minds. I can't begin to imagine what anyone here is thinking, how can I tell them anything?"

The doors whooshed open to the lobby. Lisa stepped out quickly and headed for the entrance, furious with Sam. How dare he let all those people think there was something going on between them!

She marched out to the front.

"Cab?" the doorman asked.

"Yes."

"No, the lady is with me."

Taking her arm in a firm grip, Sam led her to the side, heading toward the parking garage.

"Let me go!"

"When we get to the truck."

"I'll yell," she said, only halfheartedly pulling her arm.

"I'll yell back. Look, I know you're embarrassed by what happened, but the only way to play it was funny. We don't know any of those people and they don't know us. Why make a federal case out of it?"

"I hate logic," she murmured, walking beside him, trying to match her steps to his longer stride.

The rest of the walk was in silence. When the reached the truck, Sam put her between him and the truck releasing her arm to take her into his arms.

"I'm sorry I embarrassed you," he said, lowering his mouth to hers.

Every thought fled as she was swept away by his kiss. His lips were warm and firm, moving persuasively against hers.

Roiling emotions swept through her as she responded.

A car honked, the sound reverberating throughout the concrete structure.

Sam released her, reaching around her to unlock the truck.

"Was that a goodbye kiss?" Lisa asked when she thought she could trust her voice again.

He shook his head, reaching across her to fasten the seat belt, leaning into the truck, his face only inches from hers.

"No, I'm experimenting."

"Experimenting?"

"On how far I can go."

She closed the scant inches and kissed him sweetly. "Keep experimenting," she said in a soft voice. "I'd like to see how far you can go, too."

Lisa should be locked away or come with a big warning sign -- *danger,* Sam thought as he went around to get into the truck. Once behind the wheel, it took all his concentration to start the engine and back out of the parking stall.

Her fragrance filled the cab of the truck. He could see her from the corner of his eye and wanted to turn and take his fill of every nuance to her expression. Revel in her sparkling eyes, her smile.

He clenched his teeth tightly and focused on driving in Houston's busy traffic.

I'd like to see how far you can go, too. If that wasn't a clear sign, he didn't know what was.

They had three days together before heading back to Tumbleweed. How far could they go together in that time?

He must be crazy. Crazy about Lisa, he thought in disgust. Just like before. Crazy to be with her, to listen to her views on things, to hear her voice, touch that soft, velvety skin, taste that sweet mouth.

He almost groaned with the way his body was reacting to the thoughts. Flicking her a quick glance, he grew frustrated with her calm outlook. She gazed serenely out the window while he as about to ignite with desire.

After parking in the lot near the pens, he looked at her. "Well?"

She pulled out the show catalog.

"I have to be at this auction at ten. And then I wanted to check out some of the suppliers at the mercantile to see if we can get better pricing." She looked up, her eyes sparkling with mischief.

Sam almost reached across the bench seat and dragged her into his arms. Did she have any idea what she was doing to him?

"Want to meet for lunch or something?" she asked brightly.

"I'll see."

Her flirtatious remark floated in the air. But he was wiser this time around. A brief fling with his ex-wife was one thing.

Thinking things would change would be another.

He wasn't sure, but he thought he detected disappointment in her eyes, but she quickly dropped gaze back to the catalog.

"Well if you do, I'll meet you here around one."

He nodded. He had no intention of waiting until one

o'clock to see her again. To see if she was as interested as he was. He'd handle what he could before ten and join her for the auction. They could take the day from there.

It was shortly before ten when Sam made his way to the crowded bleachers by the pen where the ten o'clock auction was being held. Cattle bawled. A light haze of dust hung in the air. The crowd seemed to move in the same direction he wanted to go--everyone couldn't be attending the auction. This was only one of several over the course of the event.

The bleachers were already crowded. He scanned the faces, finding Lisa near the center about half way up. She was studying her catalog again. And she'd acquired a hat-- white straw with a feather headband. At least the sun would stay off her face.

It took more than five minutes to get up to where she was. Stepping over feet, brushing against ranchers already settled, he stopped beside her.

"Hi."

She looked up. The smile she gave him dazzled. "What are you doing here?"

"I finished up early so I thought I'd come to watch you spend your boss's money."

She glanced around and then with a murmured apology to the man next to her, scooted over to open a space for Sam. He sat down, hip to hip with Lisa, the warmth of her thigh heating his through the denim. It was crowded, no denying that.

He didn't mind a bit.

She shifted, and he felt every move. Her arm knocked against his.

"Sorry. It's crowded here."

"Sure is. I was surprised to find so many people for this one auction, but the whole place seems to have more people than usually attend."

"Signs of returning prosperity, I guess."

Her arm rested against his. When she shifted her leg, it brushed against his.

Sam began to wonder if this had been a good idea after all. It just mattered that every time she breathed, he felt it. That her scent seemed to surround them. That her excitement at the auction was infectious. He hadn't had such a good time in years.

Not since Lisa had left.

The thought sobered him like nothing else could have. She'd left once, would she stay in Tumbleweed this time? Or was this just a temporary measure until another job came along? One where the rancher 'd want an office manager to live on site?

The thought didn't set well.

The auction was well underway before the bull Bill Taylor had indicated he wanted was presented. Lisa sat on the edge of the seat, her numbered paddle gripped in her hand.

Sam watched her, fascinated. Every thing she did seem to fascinate him. Always had.

"We have a limit," she murmured to him.

"Of course. What is it?"

"No more than fifty thousand for the three bulls he wants."

"So roughly sixteen to seventeen grand each?"

"Except this one's so good, I could go higher with him and then try to get the others with lower bids."

"You and Bill discussed strategy?"

She nodded, leaning closer. "We played out several scenarios, but the ultimate decision will be mine. He said he couldn't second guess what might happen, so he trusts my judgment. I hope I don't mess up for him."

"You'll do fine."

He squeezed her hand, then relaxed. She didn't pull away,

just smiled at him, her attention quickly caught as the bidding process began.

Auction fever was contagious. The desire to win, to outbid the competition grew as stakes became personal. Sam watched as Lisa bid time and time again against eight or nine other ranchers. Gradually the competition dropped out and soon there were only three bidding. The price stopped jumping at five hundred dollars increments and began leaping ahead at a thousand dollars a pop.

Sam watched Lisa. She raised her paddle. The bid had risen to twenty-seven thousand. Well below her limit, but not if she was still planning to get two more bulls.

The auctioneer raised the price another grand. A man two rows down and to the left raised his paddle. The auctioneer nodded, raising the price another thousand dollars.

Lisa started to raise her paddle. Sam covered her hand, holding it in her lap.

"Let go, I need to bid."

"Think a minute, Lisa. You are almost at two-thirds your limit for the entire amount. Taylor wanted three bulls. What are you going to do if you go back with only one?"

She struggled to pull her hand free. Then stopped. Taking a deep breath she looked into his eyes, hers widening as reason took hold.

"You're right. This is getting too steep."

She looked down at the auctioneer and shook her head slightly. He began the final spiel, then slammed down the hammer. The bull had gone to someone else for thirty-four thousand dollars.

"Now I have to tell Bill why I didn't get the one he wanted."

"I doubt he wanted it at any price. Ranching's a business. Making business decisions aren't always easy, but if you follow prudent business practices, you usually come out ahead. There are plenty of good bulls. You'll get another."

"Maybe, but I'm not much for selecting which one would be best."

"Maybe I can help. Tell me what Taylor's looking for and we'll scout out some stock that'll suit."

The rest of the morning they reviewed the catalog, went to look at livestock and discussed everything from yield potential to conformation to disposition.

"Haller, good to see you." A rancher stopped by them and offered his hand.

Sam shook it and smiled. "Hank Jenkins, I haven't seen you in a coon's age. How're things going?"

"Great. Cut back on the rodeoing, though that stock cutter of mine is always in the money. What're you up to?" He tipped his hat to Lisa.

"Hank, Lisa. Hank and I have been friends for longer than I can remember," Sam said.

Hank studied Lisa for a moment, looking puzzled. "I thought I heard you two split," he said.

Sam nodded. "We did," he said shortly.

"Well, I'm glad to see that was temporary. How's that boy of yours?"

"Can't wait to ride his first bronc. Come to the ranch sometime and see him."

"Will do. Say, a bunch of us are meeting at the Sombrero just outside the south parking area for lunch. Join us?"

Sam looked at Lisa, raising an eyebrow in question.

"I'd love to stop for lunch. My mind is a jumble with all the facts and figures you've been pouring in."

The Sombrero was obviously a favorite restaurant. It was as crowded as the auction grounds had been. Hank, Sam and Lisa found the big round table with others already seated. In no time they found more chairs and squeezed in.

Once again Sam and Lisa were hip to hip. He rested his arm on the back of her chair, wondering how they'd all eat when the food came. Baskets of corn and flour tortilla chips and bowls of salsa were already piled down the center of the table. Beer was ordered, conversations flowed, changed, crossed over the table and back. The primary topic ranching.

"Bored?" he asked Lisa a few minutes later, remembering her comment about so many facts and figures.

She turned and leaned closer to be heard. "Not at all. This is more fun than I've had since --" She stopped and shrugged. "Thanks for including me," she finished.

The rim of her hat touched the rim of his. He wanted to sweep both off and cover her mouth with his and kiss her until neither could breathe.

But not in a crowded restaurant with men and women he knew and saw from time to time at rodeos and cattle shows. He'd bide his time, though his impatience was hard to contain.

I'd like to see how far you can go, told him nothing about how far she'd join him. They had three days, and he planned to make the most of every minute.

Nine

By late afternoon , Lisa felt exhausted. She'd successfully bid for one of the bulls that Bill had marked in the catalog and discussed pricing concessions with several major suppliers. The insight and suggestions Sam provided had been invaluable. But her head felt as if it were spinning.

"Ready to head back to the hotel?" Sam asked. "There are two more days to this show, you don't have to do everything the first day."

"I'm tired," she admitted, nodding her agreement, a spark of excitement flaring.

Despite the fact this was a business trip, it'd be just the two of them at the hotel, in adjoining rooms, away from the crowds, away from people who knew Sam. Away from the business at hand.

"Then let's go."

He teasingly pulled her hat lower on her forehead, shading her eyes from the sun. She wanted him to do more, to take her hand, or throw his arm around her shoulder, but he seemed content with a small teasing gesture.

She wasn't going to be the one to rush blindly out of control, she vowed as they walked to the truck. Despite her flirtatious words that morning, despite her intentions of a few days ago, she wasn't confident how far she wanted to go with this new-found friendliness.

Make haste slowly had been a favorite saying of her grandmother's. Maybe she should apply it to her own situation.

Lisa expected Sam to invite himself into her room when they reached the hotel. He didn't.

Sam waited until she opened her door, then casually asked, "Want to get supper together later?"

"I'd like that, but I didn't bring anything but jeans."

"We'll find some place around here where jeans are the attire of choice. Say seven?"

"Seven."

She smiled, waiting, but Sam just nodded and walked down the hall to his room.

She stepped inside, disappointed to see the maids had closed the connecting doors. Would he open his and knock?

Waiting by the door for several moments, Lisa was baffled when she heard nothing from his side.

Sighing softly she crossed the room, took off her hat and ran her fingers through her hair. She felt bone-tired. It was hard work buying livestock especially with someone else's money.

Pulling out her phone, she called her mom's to talk to Joey, then headed for the bathroom. A quick shower, a short nap and she'd be ready for the evening.

Every second she had her ears attuned to the room next door, but heard nothing.

The country-western bar that'd been recommended wasn't crowded when they entered shortly after seven.

"Nice," Lisa said, trying to keep the butterflies from kickboxing in her stomach.

She hadn't been on a date in more than five years. The last time they'd dated they'd been engaged to get married. Things were so different now.

"They have dancing after nine," he said, following the waitress to the tables on the left side of the huge space. To the right a long polished bar gleamed in front of a wall-size mirror. Glasses and bottles of liquor stacked up before the mirror, gleaming in the artificial light.

Between the tables and bar a wide hardwood dance floor waited, empty.

Dancing? Sam wanted to dance?

The butterflies kicked higher. Was she ready for this? Cheek to cheek, chest to chest, arms wrapped around each other? Heat skidded through her at the thought.

When they'd ordered, Sam leaned back in his chair and looked at her. "So how did you like your first solo stock show?"

"Interesting, but I wouldn't have known what to do if you hadn't been there. Bill should have come. He needs to meet other ranchers, build a network." She glanced at him shyly. "He could have learned a lot from you today."

Sam shrugged. "Have him call me if he needs help."

"Thanks, Sam. That's nice."

He smiled sardonically. "That's me, Mr. Nice."

She bit her lower lip. She hadn't always thought that. Looking away, she pushed back the memories of the past.

Tonight was not for thinking or dwelling on things not changeable. Tonight was just for fun. For the two of them.

And after two years of heartache, she wanted to experience a lot of fun!

They had steaks with all the trimmings. Her portion was regular, he had the larger size. She remembered when they'd first married, she'd tripled what she thought they'd eat and he seemed to clear his plate every time. Yet not a spare ounce of flesh ever showed. Ranching was tough physical labor and Sam worked hard.

"Want some dessert?" Sam asked when they'd finished.

She shook her head, toying with her wine glass. The band had started assembling in the small area to the back of the dance floor. Glancing around, she noticed the restaurant section had filled up.

"Want to stay?" he asked.

"Yes. I'd like that." She smiled, wondering if this feeling of euphoria would last.

They'd discussed various things over dinner, nothing controversial. The two glasses of wine had mellowed her senses and she wished the night would last forever.

By the time the band was ready to start, the place had filled up considerably, though it wasn't as crowded as the restaurant had been at lunch. At least they had their table to themselves. She almost missed the crowded condition with Sam brushing against her with every move.

Of course, dancing would change all that.

"Ladies and Gents, we'll start off with a Texas Two-step. Come on folks, time to work off that good food you just ate!"

The band began playing a lively tune.

Lisa smiled when Sam rose and offered his hand. In two seconds, they joined others on the floor and began moving around to the familiar tempo.

She and Sam had often gone dancing. She'd loved every minute. Tonight, keeping time to the music took her mind of everything but the joy of moving with the rhythm, in Sam's arms again. She'd been so lonely in Denver.

When the set of fast numbers ended and the band segued into a slow dreamy tune, Lisa didn't protest when Sam pulled her in close snuggling right up against his hard chest, putting her arms around his neck as his came around her back. It was the closest thing to heaven she'd ever felt, she thought dreamily.

Resting her forehead against his jaw, she relaxed and moved

with the music, conscious of every inch of her body pressed against his. The slow beat of his heart could be felt through their shirts. His long legs moved with hers, brushing against her thighs, causing a deep longing to bud and grow.

The dance floor was crowded, but Sam kept them from bumping into anyone. Slowly the song ended and another slow-moving tune began. The easy-going camaraderie of dinner was being replaced with an intensity she hadn't felt in years.

He tilted back his head and looked at her. "Lisa?" he said.

"Hmmm?" She opened his eyes and looked into his.

Lisa felt the deep breath he took before he spoke. "I think it's time to go back to the hotel."

Decision time.

"Okay, Sam."

They didn't speak during the short walk back, but Lisa felt like her skin had been electrified. Tingling sensations seemed to dance on nerve endings as anticipation grew by leaps and bounds all because Sam held her hand.

Or was it her imagination of what they'd do when they reached his room.

His thumb traced patterns against the back of her hand, his palm felt warm and firm against hers, the calluses from work giving his skin a slightly rough texture that heightened the sensations.

She glanced at him from time to time, his expression hiding his feelings.

When they reached their floor, Sam pulled her right past his door, stopped in front of hers.

She blinked. She thought for sure. What? That he was going to declare undying love for her and ask her to marry him again?

Nothing was resolved between them.

Lisa was hard pressed to keep from giggling. Their big seduction scene had only been in her mind. Wouldn't he love to know what she'd been thinking?

She studied Sam thoughtfully, and a warm glow filled her. Had he been as lonely as she had been for the last two years? Was he a one-woman man as she was growing to suspect she was a one-man woman?

Sam lay awake long after he'd gone to bed. He stared into the darkness, thinking about the way his life had gone. Searching for some way to reclaim the woman he wanted in his life. Not finding any.

There was too much between them.

And once she knew about Margot, Lisa wouldn't give him the time of day.

It was late when Sam finally drifted to sleep.

Lisa awoke slowly. They needed to be at the stockyard before ten when the next auction began. It was full daylight outside, so couldn't be that early. She wondered if Sam was awake. She checked the time, not yet seven. Plenty of time.

She lay in bed and thought about last night. She'd sure misread things. She hoped he didn't know she'd wanted him to stay. He obviously hadn't wanted to, he'd simply bid her good night, brushed his lips cross hers and left her to go to his own room.

It was time they had a frank conversation. She wanted more than what they'd had these last weeks.

She couldn't read him, though.

Dressing quickly, she opened the connecting door. Hesitating a moment, she softly closed it and went to call him instead.

"Haller."

135

"Are you interested in breakfast?"

"I ate a while ago. But I'll go down with you and have some more coffee."

He waited for her in the hallway and soon she had filled her plate from the breakfast buffet and sat across from him. He had a steaming cup of coffee in front of him.

"Maybe we need to talk," she said after the first pangs of hunger had been satisfied.

"About."

"Us."

"There is no us," he said, taking a sip of coffee.

"I've changed over the time we've been apart. I realize most of the reason for the divorce was my fault "

He looked at her. "I thought it was mine."

"I know I said so at the time. It was hard to live with you constantly watching me and Nick as if we were going to hop in bed together at any second. And you didn't talk to me about things when I'd ask."

"I wanted to give you the sun and moon."

"I didn't want the sun and moon, I wanted a husband--someone who trusted me and turned to me when he needed something."

Sam gave a short laugh. "That's rich, you turned to Nick every time you needed support."

"Maybe because he listened to me. Treated me as if I were an adult."

"And I didn't?"

She shook her head.

"I didn't treat you as a child," he said.

"No, but not as a partner either. Wait I know what you're going to say. You would have if I'd acted like one. I have to agree. I was too young, I think, when we got married. Too young to have a baby right away."

"You regret Joey?" Sam frowned.

"No! Never that. But if I'd thought it out, I'd have waited a bit. I was twenty-three when he was born. Looking back now, I don't feel I'd finished growing up."

"You seemed grownup to me."

"Then why wasn't I privileged enough to be treated as a partner in our marriage? Or even a confident. You know I just found out from Jennifer a stranger I've known a few weeks that you always wanted to be a vet?"

He looked at the ceiling. "It doesn't matter. I have the ranch to look after."

"The point is why didn't I know that from you?"

"It's something I thought about as a teenager. Reality stepped in when my father died and left me in charge."

"But dreams are what make us who we are. And you never shared that one with me. What does that tell you about our relationship?"

"There were things you never told me."

She reached out and her hand over one of his. "That's my point," she said softly. "We didn't do a good job."

Lisa held her breath. She wanted him to suggest they try again, doing it differently this time.

Instead, Sam nodded. "You're right. We didn't do a good job. Are you finished? I have some work to do before leaving for the stockyard."

"You go ahead. I want another cup of coffee."

Lisa watched in disbelief as he left..

"That was not the way I wanted this to end," she murmured watching him until she couldn't seem him any more.

She should have insisted he stay. No running away when things got sticky. Hadn't that been her *modis operandi* from before?

Did he not want to try? Or had she hurt him so badly it was

with her he didn't want to try?

She'd never been able to second guess the man, and it didn't look as if she had improved at all in the years apart.

Lisa debating whether to go Sam or call a cab to the stockyard. She hadn't come to Houston expecting to be in Sam's pocket every moment. Time she reasserted her own independence.

Last night hadn't change anything.

If she wanted to see what Sam had in mind, they'd have to both sit down and do some serious talking about the future.

But not today. Today, she needed to go and earn her paycheck.

She opened her door, almost stumbling when she saw Sam leaning against the wall opposite.

"Ready?" he asked.

"Yes."

They walked down to the elevator. "You could have called to ask," she said as they waited.

"I wasn't sure if you'd hang up on me or not. I think I made a tactical error in leaving before we finished that meaningful discussion."

A feeling of relief flooded.

"Actually, it's probably a good thing. This is neither the time nor the place," she said almost breathlessly.

Did that mean he did want to have a discussion?

"And the time and place would be?"

"When we finish our business here. Maybe on the ride back? We won't be interrupted or distracted unless we encounter traffic."

"And until then?" he asked.

She linked her arm with his and smiled up at him. "Until then, cowboy, I'm all yours."

The elevator doors opened. Five people stared at them.

"We'll wait for the next one," Sam said.

The door slid shut and he turned and kissed her deeply.

The day at the stockyard flew by. She successfully bid on two more bulls; one that Bill had indicated he'd like and one that Sam recommended.

She met more ranchers, and for the most part she introduced herself as just Lisa. Fending off questions of a personal nature, she asked ranching questions and learned as much as she could from the assortment of experts.

Sam declined several invitations for dinner, his eyes holding hers, rich with promise.

A promise he lived up to. They went back to the country-western bar for dinner. And danced until the band quit.

They walked back to the hotel, through the dark streets, fingers laced together as they held hands. If there were others on the sidewalk, Lisa didn't remember seeing them.

Tomorrow they'd head for home.

Or later today, she thought sleepily when she dozed off. She wouldn't have missed the trip for anything. Now if only their discussion could offer a hope of reconciliation.

She thought she was falling in love all over again with Sam Haller. And if he felt the same, maybe they could start over.

And this time, make it work.

Ten

"So when I told Bill what we'd bought, he was blown away. He said he's going to send me to all the sales and let me handle it!" Lisa said, beaming.

Sam smiled, enjoying listening to her excited recount of her conversation with her boss. They'd left Houston behind and were heading home. She'd called her boss before checking out, and was now regaling Sam with all the accolades Bill had apparently given.

He enjoyed seeing her so excited.

Was it almost time to have that discussion she'd mentioned? His gut tightened.

It was past time to tell her about Margot. Only, he wasn't sure how to go about it. He should have mentioned it at the very first. But who would have thought the first day he'd seen her in Fort Worth that she'd even give him the time of day, much less end up wanting this discussion?

He couldn't just blurt it out. Especially when he didn't know where they now stood.

He wasn't even sure what he felt or wanted.

She touched his hand.

"Are you listening to me?"

He caught her hand in his, resting them on his leg. He'd tug her closer, but seat belts prevented it.

"I heard every word. And if Taylor doesn't give you a big raise, tell him to talk to me."

She laughed. "And he wouldn't find you prejudice on my behalf?"

Sam shrugged, enjoying her laugh. It'd been a long time since he'd heard it.

Silence filled the truck for a few minutes.

"Sam?"

"Yeah?"

His heart began to pound. This was it. They had to clear up the past and the present before they could even think about a future.

"Want to talk?"

"About us?"

"Is there an us?"

"Do you want there to be?"

Lisa was silent for a moment. "I do. But I was really hurt when I left. Your distrust cut deep."

"Yeah, well maybe I won't be distrustful in the future."

"You didn't have any reason."

"I know that now," he said.

"But?"

"But what?"

"It sounds as if there's a 'but' lurking somewhere," she said.

He shook his head. "No buts. I know you and Nick weren't having an affair."

"And he's involved with Jennifer now."

"Right."

"But what if I wanted to be friends with another man. Say Bill Taylor?"

"Just friends?"

She nodded.

"Then, I'd say go for it."

"And you wouldn't get jealous?"

His lips lifted in a half-way smile. "I didn't say that. But I'll handle it better this time."

"I need you to know you don't have any reason to be jealous. I need for you to trust me totally."

"A person can't help his feelings, Lisa, only his behavior."

She sighed.

"Not willing to take the chance?" he asked.

"On what?"

"Marriage."

"I've had a lot of time to think about us over the last two years. One thing I've come to believe is we rushed into marriage."

"Of course we did, we couldn't wait."

"We don't need to rush this time. We should take things slowly. Learn more about each other. Like you said when we went to the zoo."

Only when you know more about me, you won't want to talk marriage at all, he thought grimly. How was he going to tell her? Straight out or lead up to it gradually?

"With marriage as an end?" he asked for clarification.

"Do you want to get married again to me?" she asked.

Sam almost laughed out loud. He'd never stopped wanting her in his house, riding the range with him, in his bed. The only reason he'd dated Margot was she reminded him so much of Lisa.

But there were two little children to consider this time around. Joey didn't remember their being a family or the fighting.

Sam didn't want him to be exposed to anything like that in the future. He and Lisa had better be absolutely certain they were marrying for life if they took it up again.

142

"Gee, don't rush into speech," she said, tugging her hand free.

"It's not that I don't want get married again to you," he clarified quickly. "But I'm thinking of the various ramifications."

"Like we won't make it a second time either?"

He shrugged. "There are other people to consider now."

"Joey."

"Among others," he murmured.

"Joey would be thrilled to have us back together to be a family together."

"He just wants to live on the ranch."

"That, too."

He saw her frown. He wasn't that pleased with the way the conversation was going either, but he wasn't going to make any promises he couldn't keep.

"Nick," she said flatly.

"What?"

"Nick's the other party, right? And Jennifer. Neither seem overly fond of me right now."

"They'll be living on the ranch."

"It's still your home, too."

"Nick isn't a problem."

"Could have fooled me," she muttered.

"Why?"

"He's told me in no uncertain terms to stay away from you?"

"Nick did?"

This was news to Sam. Why would his brother interfere?

"He seems to think that I'm some sort of femme fatale where you're concerned and nothing I do will be good enough."

"That's dumb."

"I wonder. Jennifer made some astute observations," she added.

"Like?"

"Like the reason for the fierce rivalry between you and Nick. How your father favored him and really came down hard on you. I knew some of that about your family. But I didn't realize how it could impact our relationship."

"And how did it?"

Sam didn't like the idea of Lisa and Jennifer discussing their relationship. What else would Jennifer let slip?

"I never should have tried to make you jealous by seeking Nick's company."

"You tried to make me jealous?" Sam asked, astonished.

She rubbed her fingers nervously on her jeans.

"Sometimes I thought you liked the ranch more than me and that if you saw someone else liked me, maybe it would make you notice me more."

He flicked her an incredulous look. "You were my wife! I was crazy about you. I never liked the ranch more. I was trying to build it up to support you in style!"

"I didn't want to be supported in style, I wanted more attention from you! I thought we were going to be partners in everything."

"We were."

"Then how come I had to find out about your dearest dream of becoming a vet from a virtual stranger?" she almost shouted.

Sam took a deep breath. "It was a kid's dream."

"Not according to Jennifer."

"So now Jennifer is the authority on my life?"

"No, not at all, but I find it interesting that you share something like that with her and not with your own wife."

"Maybe if my own wife ever asked or showed an interest, I

would have! All I can remember you wanting to do was go into town and dance."

Lisa looked at him, her eyes wide. "That's what you remember about our marriage?"

He nodded once, abruptly, his hands tightening on the wheel.

He remembered coming in from a rough day on the range and having her all dressed up to go into town. When he'd mention being tired, she'd cajole him into a quick shower and change, and off they'd go.

He also remembered one time he'd flat out refused and she'd gone with Nick.

"Water over the dam, Lisa. It doesn't matter any more. We were crazy over each other, but it burned out."

"What I remember from our marriage was that you told me that many times you were crazy about me. But now that I think about it, I don't ever remember you telling me you loved me."

"What?"

"Did you ever love me, Sam? With a bone-deep, abiding love that lasts a lifetime?"

"Is that what you felt for me? Before or after you walked out?"

"Maybe that's why we couldn't stay together. Maybe the other was merely the excuse that split us apart."

She hadn't loved him?

He didn't want to think it had only been infatuation, lust.

Was he trying to hide or had he never loved her like he should have loved a wife? Never shared things with her, never sought her advice.

She was five years younger. Had he thought she'd have nothing to offer because he was older? Or because she'd been brought up in town and not on a ranch?

How blind could a man get?

"I want you, Lisa. Anyway I can get you."

"But love?"

"I don't know."

"Me, either."

"Then let's take things slowly. See if we can discover what we really feel."

"And if it's only lust?"

He shook his head. His feelings for her went far beyond the physical. He liked her sunny outlook on life, her laughter, the sweet way she had with their son, the genuine delight she took in simple pleasures. His life had been lonely the last two years. And not just at night.

"It isn't lust," he said. "But I'm not rushing into anything again!"

"So we take it slow."

"We'll have to be circumspect in Tumbleweed. There are too many people watching ready to jump in on gossip."

"And you don't want to be seen with me?"

"Not that. But I don't want anything to get blown out of proportion or gossip to fly. We have Joey to think about this time around."

"Actually," he looked over at her, "There is someone else who will-- "

"Look out!"

He looked back at the highway just in time to see a metal dolly bouncing across the lane. He swerved the truck to avoid it, his right wheels going into the softer shoulder. Ahead of them, the truck the dolly had fallen from was pulling to the shoulder. Trying to keep the pickup under control took all Sam's efforts. Behind them they heard the sound of metal crashing against metal.

He stopped and got out. "Stay here."

Another car crashed into the first. Then another. The

sound of screeching brakes and crunching metal filled the air.

"I'm going to see if anyone needs help. Call for help."

Lisa scrambled to get her phone and dialed 911. She tried to find a mile marker to give them an idea of where they were, and ended up getting out of the truck and running ahead to one she could see.

When she turned, she was horrified. Several cars were scattered across both lanes of the highway on their side of the median strip. Some were crumpled, one seemed to be smoking. She hoped it was just radiator steam.

She hurried toward the wreckage.

All thought of their discussion fled as she searched for Sam. What if more cars slammed into the pile already several cars in length? What if he were trying to help someone and got hit himself?

There, she saw him.

Skirting the first car, she peeked inside to see if anyone needed help. By the time she reached Sam, she'd spoken to four people none seriously injured.

It was late by the time emergency vehicles arrived and the mess sorted out. Sam and Lisa gave information to the police and the owner of the rental truck which had dropped the dolly had given his statement.

"That was good driving you did," she said when they once again started for Tumbleweed. "If you hadn't avoided it, we would have been the lead vehicle in that pile up."

"The car behind us missed it, too. It was the third guy who wasn't so lucky."

"And all the ones behind him. At least a slight concussion and that twisted knee were the worst of it," she said, feeling exhausted now that the adrenaline had stopped pumping.

The rest of the trip passed without incident. Lisa halfway dozed. By the time they reached Tumbleweed, it was dark.

"Want to go to your place or your folks?" Sam asked.

"Mom's. I want to see Joey."

"Won't he be in bed by now?"

Lisa checked her watch and nodded. "But I can still look in on him. He just won't know it. Want to come in, too?"

Sam shook his head. "I'll have a million things to catch up on at the ranch tomorrow. Want to bring Joey out on Saturday or shall I come in to pick him up?"

Her heart sank. For a little while she'd thought they were making headway.

His comment sounded formal and distant. As if their three days together didn't count and they were back to square one.

"I'll bring him out."

"And stay for another picnic? It'll probably be warm enough for Joey to go wading in the creek."

"I'm sure he'll love that."

She wouldn't see Sam tomorrow. But she had work she needed to catch up on. And they'd spend Saturday together like a family again.

She wouldn't get her hopes up.

But the warmth that spread through her comforted her. Sam still wanted to see her.

Saturday was hot and muggy. Lisa couldn't blame Joey for being excited about their planned excursion to the ranch, she was excited herself.

Sam had called last night before Joey had gone to bed to talk to their son. He'd spoken to her for only a moment. But she hadn't minded she knew they'd have today together.

She prepared a lavish picnic with ham sandwiches, some of

her mother's pickles that Sam had always liked. And the cupcakes were the result of not sleeping last night due to too much excitement.

Jennifer and Nick were at some horse show this weekend, so if Sam asked her to stay for dinner, it'd be just the three of them with no other family to intrude.

She'd have to talk with Nick to come to some sort of truce if she truly wanted this relationship with Sam to grow.

Maybe enlist Jennifer's help to end the hostility. She'd see how things went today.

Sam was waiting when they drove up. He'd saddled the horses and they stood waiting patiently at the rail.

Joey scrambled from the car and ran pell mell towards his father, flinging himself into his arms. Lisa felt a twinge of envy. She'd like to do that very thing.

Instead, she put on her hat, fetched the picnic, packed well enough to withstand the horseback ride, and slowly walked over to join the two most important people in her world.

Joey was delivering his usual rapid fire recitation of what he'd been doing since he'd last seen Sam. His father nodded, then looked over at Lisa. Her breath caught. Her heart raced and the fluttery feelings she always had around Sam increased.

"I hope you brought your suit," he said when she drew closer. He leaned over and kissed her on the mouth.

She wished they were alone except Joey had been so looking forward to the day she couldn't deny him this treat.

"Yes, I did. It's hotter in town, I think. But plenty hot here, too. The water will feel great."

"I have my bathing suit on, Daddy. I just have to take off my jeans and I'm ready to go swimming!" Joey exclaimed.

"Great idea, partner. I have mine, too, so we can all play in the water."

Lisa nodded and turned to put the lunch in the saddle bag

of her mount. Her fingers almost fumbled with the task, her mind was definitely on imagining Sam in nothing but bathing trunks, his broad chest bare to the sun.

"Let's go, Daddy. I want to go swimming at the creek!" Joey said.

"I'm ready."

Just then a car came slowly down the gravel driveway that led to the house. When the driver saw them at the corral, the car changed direction.

Lisa glanced at the vehicle, then finished fastening the straps on the saddle bags. She didn't recognize car or driver.

Sam put Joey on the ground. "Go with your mom, Joey. We'll be ready to go soon."

Without a word to Lisa he went to intercept the car.

She watched, wondering who it was, hoping it wasn't some sort of ranch business that'd tie Sam up.

With Nick gone, he'd have to deal with anything that came up.

Sam leaned down, his hands on the car door, and spoke to the driver through the open window.

Lisa thought they were arguing, but she wasn't sure.

"Can we go, Mommy?" Joey asked impatiently.

"As soon as your daddy gets done. You want to ride with him, don't you?"

"I can go to the creek all by myself!"

Lisa laughed. "Not just yet. We'll wait for your daddy."

"How much longer?" Joey was impatient.

Sam straightened and glanced at Lisa. "I'll be a minute. You two want to go ahead?"

"No, we'll wait for you."

The car backed around and parked in front of the house.

The driver got out and ran up the steps into the house. Lisa didn't recognize the woman. She had long dark hair, and was wearing some sort of tunic over jeans.

Sam walked slowly over to the car, glancing back at Lisa. Feeling uneasy, she took Joey's hand.

"As soon as Daddy's guest leaves, we'll be ready to go. Do you need to go potty? There's no place to go by the creek."

"I can use a tree. Daddy does that sometimes."

Lisa smothered a grin.

"I bet he does. But I think we might as well use the toilet since we're here."

"Okay, then can we go?"

"Yes."

They walked over toward the car. Just then the screen opened and the woman walked out.

"You're a lifesaver, Sam. I needed that!"

Lisa paused.

The woman was pregnant, at least seven months along. Joey kept walking, around the car and up to his dad. Sam jerked in surprise and looked over his shoulder, his gaze meeting Lisa's.

Suddenly a frisson of fear darted down her back. His expression scared her.

"Is this Joey," the woman asked, leaning over to smile at the little boy.

"I'm Joey Haller. Who are you?"

"I'm Margot Pendarvis. Pleased to meet you, Joey." She rose and smiled at Sam. "Cute boy." Rubbing her stomach, she looked at Lisa, then at Sam.

"Nick said there was a resemblance. I guess I can see it a little. I'll be off."

Lisa walked around the car. "A friend of yours, Sam?"

Margot narrowed her eyes. "Not exactly."

Lisa looked at Sam.

He stood straight and looked her in the eye, his own dark and bleak. "Margot's the mother of my unborn child."

Eleven

"But you promised we could go to the creek," Joey wailed. "I want to go swimming!"

"Another time, Joey."

"But I want to go today. We were going to have a picnic. Why do we have to go home?" He kicked his foot against the bottom of the car seat and glared at his mother.

Lisa barely noticed. Her entire being was focused on driving, hoping she could hold together until she reached the safety of her apartment.

The mother of my unborn child.

Sam had made a baby with another woman!

The pain that ripped through her heart was almost debilitating. Gripping the wheel, she stared straight ahead, glad the traffic was light.

Hold on, she admonished herself, though she felt she wanted to scream at fate's capriciousness.

She thought she and Sam were getting closer. Even let herself daydream once or twice about their getting married again, providing Joey a home with two loving parents.

What a *fool* she'd been.

Not that the pain eased for knowing it.

"Mommy, I want to stay at Daddy's ranch."

"No, Joey. Not today."

Maybe not ever.

She should have stayed in Denver.

Would he have told her eventually?

Or would he have kept it a secret from her forever.

A small moan slipped out and she blinked her eyes against sudden tears. They were almost home. She could hold on until then.

Throwing a quick glance at her son, the pain intensified.

None of this was Joey's fault. His subdue expression, his sorrowful eyes, almost broke her heart. He had been looking forward to the day.

But that was before....

Thankfully the curb in front of the house was empty. She pulled to a stop, almost unable to release the steering wheel. Slowly she opened her cramped fingers.

"I don't want to go home," Joey muttered, crossing his arms across his chest in a perfect imitation of his father. "I want to go to the creek!"

Lisa blinked the tears again, afraid she wasn't going to win that fight.

"Joey, you can go to the creek another day. We need to get inside right now."

"No!"

Lisa gave a small hiccup and the tears flowed.

Joey's eyes opened wide.

"Mommy?" he asked, scared.

"Let's get inside," she said, brushing at her damp cheeks.

He let her unfasten the seat belt and climbed down without help.

In less than a minute they were inside. Lisa locked the door, as if someone would come charging in after her.

A sob burst forth.

That was dream stuff. Sam hadn't come after her before.

She'd be a bigger idiot to think he'd come now.

Especially when he was having a baby with someone else.

"Mommy, are you hurted?" Joey asked, patting her leg, looking worried.

"Oh, Joey," she knelt, and scooped him into her arms, breathing in the little boy scent of him, burying her face against his hair and letting the tears fall.

He stayed still for a few minutes, then grew restless.

"Sorry, sweetie pie," she said, falling back to sit on the floor, leaning against the door. Burying her face in her hands, she let the tears fall.

Her phone rang.

Lisa ignored it.

"Mommy, your phone is ringing," Joey said. "Should I answer it?"

She shook her head. She couldn't talk to anyone now.

Maybe never.

Secretly, somewhere deep in the recesses of her heart, she'd always thought she and Sam would get back together. Hadn't that been the real reason she'd returned to Texas. Meeting at the Fort Worth stock sale had just sped up the process.

Now she wished she'd never left Denver. Loneliness and hope offered more than reality.

Joey patted her shoulder. "Don't cry, Mommy," he said.

She dashed away the tears and tried to smile at him.

"I'll be okay. Why don't you go in your room and play with your cowboys? I'll go wash my face."

Biting her lip, she tried to control the sobs and succeeded until he was out of the room.

Wearily pushing herself to her feet, she went into the bathroom and ran cool water. Soaking a cloth, she pressed it against her eyes, letting the hot tears continue.

She'd cried for weeks after leaving Sam. But that pain

couldn't compare with this.

Her phone rang again.

She ignored it.

Returning to Tumbleweed had been a mistake.

Let's have a talk, clear the past. How dumb. He had no intention of clearing the past to make a future with her. Why hadn't he told her so?

If she lived to be a hundred, she'd never understand the man!

Lisa rinsed the wash cloth again and went to lie down in her bed.

She never wanted to face anyone again.

By mid afternoon, she'd regained some of her equilibrium.

She'd fed Joey lunch and talked him into taking a nap. She lay down beside him and told a story until he fell asleep.

Closing her own eyes, she wished she could find oblivion in sleep. But she kept seeing Margot Pendarvis and hearing Sam tell her over and over that Margot was the mother of his unborn child.

She'd have liked to have another child with Sam. She'd thought once that she'd be the mother of all his children.

The knowledge that she wasn't and never would be, cut deep.

When the tears came again, she slipped from Joey's side and went back to her own room.

By Sunday evening , Lisa was exhausted. She'd taken Joey into Dallas to a park to let him run off his excess energy. He'd constantly whined about wanting to go to the creek. She'd told him he'd go some day soon.

Sam was still his father and still would have to see him.

But the way she felt right now, she didn't want to ever see Sam again.

Yet the mere thought made her stomach churn.

Never to see his eyes crinkle in laughter? Never to hear that sexy voice talking to her quietly in the night? Never to feel those strong arms around her or hear his views things.

She didn't think she could bear it.

Joey was asleep. Lisa sat on the sofa, gazing off into the dark. She was too tired to even get up to go to bed. Maybe if she sat a little longer

The knock on the door startled her. After a moment it was repeated, harder this time.

Crossing to the door, she looked through the peephole. Nick.

Leaning her head against the wood, she wondered if she was up to this?

"Lisa, open up." He pounded on the door again.

Afraid he'd wake Joey, not to mention annoy the neighbors, she unfastened the bolt and opened the door.

He looked at her in disgust.

"You look awful," he said, stepping in beside her and flipping on the lights.

"Come in, why don't you?" she said closing the door behind him.

Turning in the center of the living room, he crossed his arms over his chest and stared at her.

"Want to tell me what's going on?" he asked.

"Why don't you ask Sam?"

"Sam looks worse than you do. He says you met Margot."

"The mother of his unborn child?" she snapped.

"So, what do you care? You left him! You had your chance and you threw it away. What's it to you if he tries to find some happiness with someone else?"

His eyes narrowed as he waited for her response.

Lisa swallowed. Put that way, she had no cause for feeling the way she did.

But it wasn't that way.

"He could have told me."

Nick shrugged. "He would have eventually, a kid's a hard thing to hide."

"Is he marrying Margot?"

Nick shook his head. "I'm sure he asked her. But she has other things she wants to do in life. It was all he could do to convince her to carry the baby to term and let him raise it."

"Let him raise it?"

"Sam plans to raise the child. Margot doesn't want anything to do with it once it's born."

Lisa blinked. How could anyone not want a baby? Sam's baby?

"I didn't know."

She walked to the sofa, sitting on the edge as her knees threatened to give way.

"Yeah, well you might have learned something if you'd answered your phone or come to the door today."

She looked up. "We were in Dallas today."

"Sam tried to call you a dozen times yesterday. With Jennifer gone and you not answering, he drove into town just to make sure you got home safely. He was worried about you."

"Why? I'm sure he has other things to worry about, like Margot."

"Margot's doing fine."

Nick unfolded his hands and tipped his Stetson back on his head. He sat on the chair near the sofa and stretched out his long legs. Lisa's heart skipped a beat--he reminded her so much of Sam.

Looking at her, he tilted his head slightly.

"So, tell me Lisa. What did you expect Sam to do, carry the torch for you the rest of his life?"

"I don't care what he does."

"That's obvious. You left him, remember?"

"He drove me away!"

Nick looked at the ceiling for a minutes. "Actually, I think we drove him into acting like a wild man." He met her gaze. "I did it to get a rise out of him. Why did you?"

"What do you mean?"

"Every time things didn't go your way, you hightailed it to my place to dump on me. Sam found you there time after time. I should have barred the door. But I let you come in--it was fun to watch him get jealous. At least at first. But by the time I realized what was happening, you two had split. I have to take part of the blame."

Lisa sighed, looking down at her hands.

"It was my fault. Marriage didn't turn out to be exactly what I thought it'd be. Before we knew it, we had a baby on the way and then I was pretty much stuck at the house to take care of Joey. I thought marriage would be glamour and fun, and it turned out to be work."

"So you left."

She nodded.

"I shouldn't have. My only explanation is that I was too immature to realize what I had. And to know how to hold on to it."

Tears threatened again. She'd done this. There was no one else to blame.

"Sam was devastated when you left especially when you moved so far away. Maybe he'd have handled it better if you'd stayed in town. At least he could have seen you, seen Joey. But to go so far and allow him to see Joey only a couple of times a year, that was hard, Lisa."

She nodded. It'd been hard for her, too.

"He about went crazy when he realized you weren't coming back." Nick rubbed his jaw. "We got into one hellacious fight."

She looked up at that. "I didn't know."

Shrugging, he shook his head. "No reason you should have. Sam went wild, working hours that would have killed another man trying to get exhausted enough to sleep at night. Drinking, carousing. Did you ever take a look at Margot? A good look?"

"I can see she's pregnant."

"She looks like you. That's why he started dating her, because she reminded him of you."

Lisa stared at Nick, tightening her lips.

After a moment, she asked, "Why are you here?"

"I wanted to talk to you. Maybe make you see things from someone else's point of view. You sure turned out to be different from the way I thought about you in high school."

"We aren't in high school any longer."

"No, and from the mess you and Sam have made of things, I'm glad we stopped seeing each other a long time ago."

Lisa looked away so he couldn't see the hurt his words caused.

He rose. "I don't know if this does any good, but it helped me get it off my chest. Cut him some slack, Lisa. He loves Joey and wants to see him. I'd say he's crazy about you, though why he would be after the way you've treated him is beyond me. But remember this--when he was dating Margot, he was free and single. He'd been dumped by the woman he'd chosen to be his wife. He had no ties to you, no loyalties, nothing. It's too bad about what happened, but he'll love that new baby as much as he loves Joey. And the kid will have a great home. If you two have something going, then it'll be up to you to get beyond this."

"It's not something to get beyond." Lisa said through stiff lips.

"If you met a man for the first time today and knew he had two kids, what would you do? Cut yourself off from any relationship because he had a past?"

He crossed the room, and opened the door.

Glancing at her, he said, "This is Sam's week with Joey. I'll be picking him up in the morning."

With that he stepped outside and closed the door.

Lisa didn't move.

The final click sounded loud in the silence.

Monday, Lisa bid Joey goodbye when Nick came to pick him up. The little boy was delighted to be going to the ranch. Lisa wished she could keep him home, but the precedence had been set. He spent every other week with his father.

And soon a new brother or sister.

She tried to ignore the thought, but it persisted. Driving to the Taylor ranch, she mentally listed all the tasks awaiting her, focusing on something else beside Sam Haller and the revelation she'd learned on Saturday.

Joey scrambled out of the truck, running toward his father. "Daddy! Can we go to the creek today?" He flung himself around Sam's legs, looking up beseechingly.

Sam ruffled his hair and shook his head. "Not today, partner. I've got work to do."

"When?"

"Soon." He looked up as Nick ambled over. "Did you see her?"

"Yeah. She's fine. She took Joey to Dallas yesterday."

Sam nodded, and turned back to the boy. "Want to help Jose with the leather today?"

"I want to go to the creek."

"Another time. Work first."

"You sound like Dad," Nick commented as he walked with the two of them toward the barn.

"Jeez, hit a man when he's down."

"The old man wasn't all bad, you know."

"So you say."

Nick paused by the stall containing his horse. "If it helps any she looked bad, her eyes all puffy and red."

Sam barely paused in his stride, the slight hitch the only sign he gave that he'd heard.

Lisa had been crying. He was the cause. He'd known all along her finding out about Margot would change things. And the way she'd discovered it couldn't have been worse.

Why hadn't he told her when she'd first moved back?

Because of her reaction.

He'd known how she'd take it. And he'd wanted those few weeks with her.

For a few days, he'd thought he might have a future with her again.

"Daddy, when can we go to the creek?" Joey asked.

"Maybe we'll swing by tomorrow on the way out to check that part of the ranch, want to do that?"

"And go swimming?"

"We'll see," Sam said absently, remembering the aborted picnic.

They'd all had on suits, planned a fun day by the creek until Margot had arrived.

"Stay with Jose, now, and help him out, okay, partner?" Sam said when they reached the tack room.

"Okay. Hi Jose, we're going to the creek tomorrow."

161

"So? Going to catch some fish?"

Joey looked up at Sam his eyes wide. "There're fish in the creek?"

"Not where we swim. Maybe when you're older, we'll see if we can catch some."

Joey smiled happily and went to stand by the old cowboy.

Sam spun around and headed for the million and one tasks that never ended on a ranch. Once again he was plunging into work to try to keep heartache at bay.

Was there anything he could say to Lisa to have her listen to him? Have her understand?

And what? Ask her to take on another woman's child?

She seemed content with her life the way it was.

He'd have to get used to that.

The day seem to drag by for Lisa. Bill asked her twice if she felt all right. Smiling brightly both times, she assured him she was. The last thing she needed was to go back to that empty apartment a moment before she needed to. She missed Joey. Just Joey.

But she couldn't stay away forever. Once home, she changed into shorts, fixed herself some comfort food and went to lie down. She didn't sleep, but dozed off and on, and thought about Sam and Margot, and the mess she'd made of all their lives.

She wished she could have had some of the knowledge she'd acquired over the last two years back when she first got married. Nick was right. She had thrown away the best relationship she'd probably ever have.

She'd released Sam from any and all commitment with the divorce. He'd been free to see whomever he pleased.

The knowledge hurt.

She'd childishly wanted him to come after her, demand she return home. How juvenile could she be. He'd treated her as an adult by respecting her wishes.

Only they hadn't really been her wishes.

Now what was she going to do about it?

Wednesday, Lisa called the ranch to talk to Joey. Her voice was cool and distant when she requested to speak with her son. She didn't want to talk to Sam.

When she hung up some time later, she was only marginally happier having spoken with Joey. She'd thought Sam might say something at least offer an explanation or ask to see her.

Not that anything he'd say would help.

Nick had pleaded his case adequately. It changed nothing.

Restless and a bit lonely, she left the apartment and went to sit on the porch. A couple walked hand in hand on the sidewalk, waving as they passed the house. Lisa smiled and waved back. From the distance, they'd never know the effort it took to smile.

She rocked a while, letting the quiet night sooth her. Crickets sounded in the heat, and she tried to remember how to figure out how hot it was by their cadence. But it'd been so long ago when she'd known that and other things pressed in on her now.

A familiar truck pulled up and stopped. Lisa watched as Nick climbed out and went around to let Jennifer out. They laughed as something and headed up the walkway.

"Oh, Lisa." Jennifer said when she spotted Lisa on the porch.

"Good evening," she said, feeling awkward. Once she and Nick had been best friends, girlfriend and boyfriend. Even after they had gone in other directions, they'd stayed friends.

163

Now she only felt embarrassed to be around him. His words echoed.

Jennifer turned to Nick and murmured something, then kissed him.

"See you tomorrow," he said easily. Turning, he headed back to the truck without a word to Lisa.

Jennifer came up and sat in a rocker beside Lisa.

"Isn't this weather gorgeous? Warm in the day, but so pleasant in the evenings. I want Nick to get some rockers so we can sit out on nights like this."

Lisa smiled, amused for the first time in what seemed like ages. "I can't see Nick sitting out on a porch at least not before he's seventy."

Jennifer laughed. "I know, but I keep asking. Sometimes just by plugging away at something, you can get what you want."

"But not always," Lisa murmured.

"I'm sorry about you and Sam," she said after a minute.

Lisa tensed. She didn't want to discuss the situation with anyone especially someone she hardly knew.

"I know, it's not any of my business. But Sam's going to be my brother-in-law soon and I like him a lot. I think he's gotten a rotten deal."

"Because of me," Lisa said.

"Yes, if you want me to be honest. What do you want, Lisa?"

Lisa looked at her in the dark. "Doesn't everyone want to be happy?"

"And how will you accomplish that? By blaming him for being human? You left. He tried to find happiness with you gone."

"I wish him well, then, with Margot."

"I don't think so," Jennifer said. "I think you want Sam for yourself."

Lisa looked out across the street wishing she'd stayed inside. She didn't need this. The ache in her heart hasn't ease a bit since Saturday.

"We don't always get what we want."

Jennifer reached out and patted her hand. "I know. But sometimes we can if we don't give up. I bet I have my rocking chairs by next summer. I bet you could have Sam this summer if you'd forgive and let him know how you feel. He's crazy about you, always has been from what I hear."

"I want love," Lisa said stubbornly. She looked at Jennifer. "I've thought a lot about it over the last week or so. I don't ever remember him saying he loved me. He did say he was crazy about me. What does that mean?"

"Did you ever ask him? You know guys have a hard time sometimes saying what they mean. And from what Nick says, there wasn't a lot of love going around out there when their father was alive. Maybe Sam doesn't know how to say it. Or maybe he doesn't even recognize it when he's knee deep in love. Give him a chance, Lisa. Don't let pride and hurt feelings prevent you from having what you want in life."

"So what do you suggest I do, ride out there and tell Sam it doesn't matter that he made a baby with someone else, that I want to try marriage again?" Lisa asked hotly.

"Only if that's what you want," Jennifer said softly. "But if you're sitting here thinking he's going to ride up one day on a white charger and sweep you off your feet, you'll be an old lady before you realize it'll never happen. That man's been knocked down more than he can get up, I'm thinking."

"I'm not the one who made him sleeping with Margot."

"No?" Jennifer asked gently.

Twelve

Sam tucked Joey into bed, listening as he chattered about his mother. He'd left the room after giving Joey the phone that evening. Lisa obviously hadn't wished to talk to him.

After Joey was asleep, he debated calling her, but didn't have a clue what he'd say.

As far as she was concerned, his being with another woman was the final straw.

And he had no doubt she saw it as a betrayal.

Wouldn't you have? a voice inside asked. What if Lisa had become pregnant with another man's baby. The thought burned in his gut. He'd have hated it.

Could he have gotten past it to see what they could make together? He didn't know.

The admission eased some of his anger. If the situation was reversed, he'd probably react the same.

Talking about it wouldn't change anything.

There was nothing left to do but go on. Nothing had changed. They were divorced. And he was about to become a father again.

Sunday morning, Lisa dressed for church in a pale blue skirt and white eyelet top. It was growing hotter every day. Before long summer would arrive full blast.

She missed Joey.

Jennifer had come down Friday night to say Sam and Joey were joining her at a horse show in which she was participating. Joey wanted to see her ride. It meant a day's delay in Joey's returning home, but Lisa wouldn't deprive him of the event.

Jennifer had invited Lisa as well, but she'd quickly turned her down.

Sam hadn't phoned to say when to expect them. She'd called her mother and arranged to join her parents at the church and then go back with them for lunch.

Leaving a note on the door for Sam, she walked to the church she'd attended all her life.

The large interior was cool and crowded with friends and neighbors. She spoke with several as she made her way up the aisle to where her parents were already seated.

"Where's Joey?" her mother asked when Lisa slipped in beside her.

"Still at Sam's. He's coming home later today."

"In time to join us for lunch?"

Lisa started to shake her head when she heard, "Hi, Mommy."

Joey ran between the pews and sat beside her with a bounce, beaming up at her. "We surprised you."

Lisa looked up into Sam's hard stare. Her breath caught. He wore a sports jacket and bolo tie with a western stitched white shirt. The slacks were a change from jeans. His boots had a high polish. He held his hat in one hand.

"Lisa," he said as greeting, sitting beside Joey.

"What are you doing here?" she whispered.

"I brought my son to church. Do you have a problem with that?"

She stared at him, feeling the churning emotions that hadn't eased all week threaten to overwhelm her. She wanted to reach out and touch him, make some connection.

Conversely, she wanted him to leave and never come around her again.

Her mother leaned over. "Hi, Joey, Sam. Glad y'all could make it. We're going back to our place afterward for lunch, join us?"

"Mother!"

Lisa hadn't told her mother about Sam and Margot. But she couldn't stand the normalcy of everything. Her world had tilted when she'd learned the news.

Sam shook his head, his gaze holding Lisa's. "Joey'd like it, I'm sure. But I need to talk to Lisa. If you wouldn't mind taking him, that'd give us some time alone."

"I don't want to talk to you," Lisa said.

"Tough. We need to talk and we will."

She blinked and looked to the front of the church. Somehow the emotions that bubbled weren't conducive to peace on earth good will toward men. Especially not to the man next to her.

The sermon seemed interminable. Normally she enjoyed the minister's lesson, today she was too conscious of Sam sitting only a few feet away. Of the revelation of last Saturday. Of the aching hurt that wouldn't fade.

Joey squirmed impatiently a time or two. She was annoyed to find that Sam's merely touching him gently on the shoulder was enough to settle him down.

Finally it was over.

"If you change your mind, come over," Margaret said to Sam, holding Joey by the hand. She glanced at Lisa and back to Sam.

"I hope your discussion's fruitful."

Lisa's dad shook hands with Sam and followed after his

wife and grandchild.

Sam took Lisa's arm in a firm grip.

"I don't have anything to say to you," Lisa said in a low voice as they joined the crowd making its way down the aisle to the back of the church. She refused to draw attention to them by trying to tug her arm free.

Not that she'd need to. People were already noticing the two of them and whispering. She could just imagine what they were saying.

Color flooded her cheeks.

"I have plenty to say to you. And I'm sure you must have a question or two."

Sam seemed oblivious to others in the church. His attention was solely on Lisa.

"I think you said it all last Saturday."

Sam didn't reply. The tightening of his hand was the only indication he gave that he heard her.

Walking out into the bright sunshine, Lisa wished she'd brought a hat or something to shade her face. Or dark glasses to shield herself from Sam's gaze.

Instead, she felt as if she were in a spotlight.

"Where did you want to have this talk?" she asked, stopping to one side on the crowded walkway.

"Some neutral place."

"Right here?"

"I think this might take longer than you think."

"We really have nothing to talk about."

She didn't want to talk. She wanted to scurry home and shut the door on the world.

He turned to face her, blocking her from the crowd dispersing behind him.

"I want you to marry me, Lisa."

"What?"

His sardonic smile mocked. "I thought that'd get your attention."

"Is that a joke?" she asked suspiciously.

The smile faded. "No. I'm deadly serious. I think we should get married again."

"No."

She looked away, afraid of what he might see if she didn't.

"Don't dismiss the idea out of hand."

"Are you crazy? You sleep with some other woman, make a baby and then want me to marry you?"

He took a deep breath. "I knew this wouldn't be easy."

"Easy, nothing. It's dumb, stupid, ludicrous. I wouldn't marry you if--"

He put a finger over her lips. "Don't say it. Don't say anything. I want to talk to you and you're going to listen if I have to hog tie you to do it."

She opened her mouth to refute his assertion, then snapped it shut.

Maybe she'd listen to him. Just to hear what he had to say. To see if it'd ease the ache in her heart at all.

"Okay."

He headed for his truck, parked up the block. The pounding of her heart was because of the heat, she decided as she hurried to keep pace beside him. Not in reaction to his touch, to the feel of his fingers on her skin. The tingling was an interruption in her blood circulation, not awareness, not a joyful delight in his touch.

He drove to the park in the center of town. There were benches scattered beneath the tall century old oak trees, affording shade and some privacy as they were spaced wide enough apart conversations couldn't be overheard. Sam chose the one farthest from the playground area. Sitting down, he half turned to look at Lisa.

She sat and stared ahead, refusing to meet his eyes. Making her displeasure as clear as she was able.

"I think getting married would be perfect," he began.

That caused her to swivel around and glare at him. "I don't see it that way."

"If you want a wife, why not ask her?"

He hesitated a moment.

Lisa closed her eyes and sighed. Obviously he already had. Margot must have turned him down.

Opening them again, she hoped the tears she felt welling wouldn't fall. He'd asked another woman to marry him. To share his life.

"I didn't even date in the last two years," she said softly.

"And I went on a bunch of dates trying to get you out of my mind. Including a whole series with Margot. Your leaving left a big hole in my life. I was trying to fill it up. Nothing worked."

Lisa felt the familiar guilt mixed with sorrow.

"We should have worked harder on our marriage when we had the chance," she said.

"Yes."

She waited, but he assigned no blame.

"I should have," she said.

He shrugged. "It takes two. The way I see it, we've learned from our mistakes. We wouldn't make them again."

"I don't think I could ever marry you again, Sam."

"Because of Margot?"

She nodded. "I'm really hurt. Not that you dated. Not even that you slept with someone else. You were free to do whatever you wanted. But that you made a baby..."

"I can't change that, Lisa. And if you can't live with it, you can't. The child's mine. Margot doesn't want anything to do with it once it's born. So we come as a packaged deal. You're right. I was free to do whatever I wanted."

He paused a moment, as if marshaling his thoughts. "I never thought you and I'd have a chance again, but seeing you in Fort Worth, and then our spending time together since then, I believe we've got something, sweetheart. You can't deny the feelings that sizzle between us."

"Sex isn't everything."

"It isn't only sex and you know it."

Lisa refused to admit to that.

"You're a wonderful mother. Look at how well you're bringing up Joey. You love kids, I bet this baby would wrap itself right around your heart."

"You ask too much."

He sat back on the bench and stretched his long legs out in front of him, stuffing his hands into his pockets.

"Maybe I do. I want you back, Lisa. I'd give you anything I have."

The tears eased slid down her cheeks. The lump in her throat was impossible to swallow. It was too late.

"I guess I thought it was fate when I saw you again in Fort Worth. Maybe it was--capricious and mean. I thought I'd put you behind me. That I could go on fine the way I was. One glimpse of you and I knew I'd been kidding myself."

She reached out, hesitating before touching him. Clenching her hand into a fist, she let it fall in her lap.

"I can't do it, Sam. I'm sorry about everything. The divorce was my fault and I'd change it if I could. But you're asking too much."

And nowhere had he mentioned love. What kind of marriage would it be without that primary ingredient?

He looked up at the branches of the trees. The silence was punctuated by the distant shouts and laughter of children playing on the swings and slides at the playground.

A soft breeze ruffled the leaves, soughing through the branches.

"Want to hear about Margot?"

Lisa lifted a shoulder half-halfheartedly. "I guess." Might as well know it all.

"I started dating her last fall." He threw her a quick glance. "She reminded me of you a little."

"Nick said that."

"You and Nick are speaking now?"

"He came by to lecture me, if you call that speaking."

"Interesting. Do any good?"

She shook her head. "Go on."

"Margot isn't you. She looks a little like you with that auburn-brownish hair and blue eyes. And she has a fun sense of adventure. It wasn't meant to be. She doesn't like ranching or horses or anything to do with cattle. So for an occasional date, we did fine. When I tested the waters for something more, she backed off quickly enough."

He'd been searching for a replacement wife.

What did she expect, that he'd remain celibate the rest of his life?

Sam was young and virile and deserved to have a full, rich life. Had she truly expected him to martyr himself because of her?

Childishly, she rather thought she had.

"An occasional date doesn't end up pregnant."

"We went to a Thanksgiving Day party with a bunch of married friends. Everyone was talking about family and traditions and I had asked you if Joey could come for the weekend and you'd said no. I was mad and lonely and--"

He took off his hat and rubbed his fingers through his hair, resetting the Stetson.

"I got drunk, Margot got drunk and the next thing I knew

two months later she's telling me we're parents-to-be and she wants nothing to do with the baby."

"Hard to walk away from," Lisa murmured dryly.

Sam nodded, his eyes dark as he gazed into hers. "She agreed to have the child when I said I'd take care of all expenses and raise it myself."

Lisa swallowed hard.

Would things have been different if she'd come home last Thanksgiving? Her parents had urged her to bring Joey to share a family celebration. She'd stubbornly refused.

"That baby will need a mother, Lisa. Think about it, won't you? I'm still crazy about you."

"You want a mother for your new baby."

"And a mother for Joey. And a family. You know I didn't have much growing up. Wouldn't you like for our son to have a mother and father living together? He'll have a little brother or sister soon. Wouldn't it be better for them to grow up together? Making memories, setting traditions?"

It was what she'd wanted. Could she take it without love? Find it in her heart to love a child that wasn't her own?

But was Sam's.

The hurt threatened to drown her.

"Just think about it, Lisa. Will you?"

"It'll be hard to not think about it," she said with some asperity. She'd done nothing all week except think about Sam and Margot and Joey. And the new baby.

And lie in bed nights remembering all the times they'd shared together. Longing for that closeness, that feeling of belonging. Could she marry for that? Would it be enough for the long years ahead?

"Come on, I'll take you to your parents. Unless you want to stop somewhere for lunch?"

She shook her head.

"You might still be in time for dessert at your folks."

The short drive was accomplished in silence. Sam pulled to a stop in front of the Ballentine's house and looked at her.

"Can I see you this week?"

"I don't think so," Lisa said, fiddling with the shoulder strap of her bag.

Just then her mother ran out of the house and up to the car, her eyes worried.

Lisa opened the door. "Mom?"

"Do you have Joey?" she asked in agitation.

Lisa's heart skipped a beat. "Joey? He went home with you and Dad."

"He's gone. Your father's out looking for him, as well as the neighbors. I hoped maybe you'd found him." She looked frantically around. "I don't know where he went. Or why."

Sam got out of the truck and came around to Margaret. Gently taking her shoulders he turned her to face him.

"Tell us what you do know," he said firmly. Lisa bumped his arm trying to get closer.

"When did he leave, Mom?"

"We got home from church and he changed into shorts. Then he asked to go to the creek. We said no, we had to eat lunch. I was in the kitchen preparing the meal and your father was on the front porch reading the paper. You know how he likes to do that in the nice weather. We thought Joey was playing in his room. When I called him for lunch, he wasn't there. We searched everywhere. I don't think he's hiding, I think he's gone off."

"To the creek," Sam said, looking down the street.

"He couldn't do that. The creek's on the ranch property, miles from here," Lisa said.

Panic threatened. She had to do something. Her little boy was missing! Wandering who knew where!

175

"A kid wouldn't have any concept of distance."

"We've got to find him!"

"We will, honey. We will. Margaret, which direction did George take?"

"He and Ben Lattimore went that way," she pointed down the street. "Bud Hazelwood and Thomas Ayers went that way." She pointed in the opposite direction. "I'm so sorry. I never would have left him alone for a second if I'd thought he'd do something like this."

"It's not your fault, Mom," Lisa said, impatient to be off. "Joey knows better. He's probably feeling a lot more adventuresome now after spending so much time on the ranch."

"Lisa, stay with your mom. I'll have a look and see what I can find. There's no way he could get through the back yard, is there? I could try that direction, rather than just follow where the others are searching."

"There's the old gate. But I don't think he could reach the latch," Lisa said, already starting to run to the back yard. Sam right beside her.

"What gate?"

"We used it as kids. It opens on to a field. Sally and I played there lots when we were little. It was the wild open spaces for us. But I don't think--"

They came to the section of fencing where a gate stood opened ten inches or more.

Lisa yanked it wider and dashed through, scanning the area. A wide open field stretched several acres in front of her. A thick copse of trees grew in the distance to the left and rocky rough terrain to the right marked the edge of an arroyo. The deep ditch had been carved from the ground over the years by flash floods. The field was lush with fresh spring grass and wildflowers. No sign of a little boy could be seen.

"Looks like he might have gone this way," Sam said, kneeling down to study the grass. "See the path of bent grass? Someone or something came through here not too long ago."

"Someone? Do you think he was kidnapped?"

"No, I think he wandered off searching for the creek. He talked about it all week." Sam rose and looked at Lisa. "We didn't get our picnic last Saturday and I think it meant more to him than we thought."

"We've got to find him, Sam," she said urgently, starting across the field. He caught her arm.

"Wait a minute. Stay with your mom. I'll bring him home if he went this way."

"I'm going." She shrugged free and resumed walking briskly.

"Your shoes won't hold up," he warned as he began to follow the direction of the faint tracks.

"Then I'll walk barefooted," she snapped. She wasn't going to let a pair of sandals keep her from searching for her baby.

They walked in silence across the field. The faint trail Sam was able to follow rambled, heading toward the rocks, but never in a straight direction.

Lisa's heart froze in fear. She couldn't lose her son, her precious Joey. She loved him. He had to be all right.

Sam looked over and reached out a hand. Gratefully, she gripped it tightly with one of her own.

His calmness in the face of the possible tragedy was reassuring. His hand a comfort and lifeline.

"Joey!" he called. They waited for a moment, Lisa holding her breath to hear better. Nothing but the soft sound of the wind in the long grass.

"If he went to the rocks, he could have fallen down the hillside and hit his head," Lisa said, wanting to run, but knowing she'd do better if they followed Joey's tracks. No sense getting to the edge of the arroyo if he'd veered left or right.

"He's pretty smart for a little guy," Sam said. They found a patch of clover, where a bunch of flowers lay scattered. Sam pointed to them. "He stopped to pick some, then decided to let them lay. Wonder what he was thinking?"

"We made a clover flower chain once, maybe he thought he could do it and when he couldn't he gave up." Lisa said, more for something to do than that it mattered. "Joey!" she called.

They reached the edge of the bluff and looked left and right. In the distance a small figure was sitting on the edge, feet dangling over.

"Joey!" Lisa began to run. In only seconds, she was close. Sam reached out and stopped her.

"Joey?" he said calmly, his arm a tight band around Lisa's waist.

"Let me to go him."

"No, the edge looks insubstantial. Your additional weight could cause it to break away."

She took a shaky breath and examined the terrain. Sam was right. From their angle she could see the lower part of the bluff had been undercut in a recent storm. It 'd be a long fall if the edge gave way.

"Joey?"

"Hi Mommy, Daddy. I camed to the creek. But there's no water."

"This isn't our creek, son," Sam said calmly. "Come on back with us and we'll go to the creek. The one on the ranch has water."

"Can Mommy come, too?"

"Of course," Lisa said. "We'll have fun. Come away from the edge now, baby."

"I'm not a baby!" Joey stood and glared at his mother. "I'm big. Ask Daddy."

"Yes, you are. Come on now and we'll go to the creek."

"Okay." He turned to fling a stone as far out as he could, the movement crumbling the edge.

"Watch out!" Lisa called, startling the little boy. The earth began to shift.

Sam darted forward, reaching Joey just as a section gave way and slid down into the gully.

"Sam!" Lisa stared in horror as both her son and husband disappeared.

Caution reigned. She eased toward the edge, peering over to see if they were all right. It was a twenty foot drop to the bottom. The ground seemed to move beneath her feet and she quickly moved back. Going up a few yards to where the edge was more sturdy, she looked over again.

Joey was held against Sam's chest, moving and struggling to get up. Sam wasn't moving at all.

"Joey, are you two okay?" she called down.

"Daddy's sleeping," Joey said, scrambling to his feet. "And I got an owie on my leg."

Lisa saw him examine his leg, sure it was scraped from their fall.

Why wasn't Sam moving?

Her heart caught. "Sam?"

"He's sleeping mommy. Can we go to the creek now?" Joey called up.

He seemed so tiny on the floor of the wide arroyo. But she could tell he was fine. It was Sam she worried about.

Eyeing the edge, she didn't find a place that offered a trail to the bottom. The sheer rock-studded wall looked impenetrable.

"Mommy, Daddy's bleeding!" Joey called up after trying to wake Sam.

Panic flared anew. He'd hit his head in the fall. Oh, lore,

Lisa thought, don't let him be dead. Not with all that was still between them.

Not before she'd had a chance to tell him that she loved him!

Love?

"Gee, your timing stinks as usual," she murmured as the full realization of her feelings swept through her.

She loved Sam. Had from the first. Separated by time and distance hadn't erased that love.

Even knowing about the new baby hadn't extinguished it.

She loved him and now she was afraid she wouldn't get the chance to tell him.

"Joey, I can't come down. I have to go get grandpa help. Can you stay with Daddy?"

"Okay Mommy. Guess what? There's water here after all."

"Water?" Lisa looked closely. There was a small stream in the center of the arroyo. Looking toward the mountains, she noticed the storm clouds.

If they got too much rain in the mountains, this arroyo could fill with water. Flash floods weren't the only kind of runoff, a steady rise from a distant storm could threaten to drown her family if they didn't get to higher ground.

"If the water gets higher, Joey, climb up as high as you can," Lisa called, fear beating in her heart. She didn't want to leave, but she couldn't do anything herself. She had to have help.

"Mommy loves you," she called.

Joey smiled and waved. He plopped down beside Sam and patted his arm.

"I'll be as quick as I can, Joey. Stay with Daddy."

"Okay."

Lisa ran like she'd never run before. Her sandals rubbed blisters. Half way across the field a strap snapped. She kicked off the shoe, taking time to discard the other one and began running again. The grass was cool against her feet, but she scarcely noticed.

The field seemed miles long. Was the water rising? Had Sam regained consciousness? Please lord, let them be all right, she chanted as she ran as fast as she could.

The fence came into view. Her breath was labored and her legs burning, but she didn't slow her pace at all.

Slamming through it, she raced to the house.

"Mom! Mom! Is Dad back? I need help."

"Lisa?" Margaret appeared at the back door, holding it wide for her. "Heavens, did you find him?"

"Sam's hurt. He and Joey are in the arroyo and there's water," she gasped, leaning over to catch her breath. "We've got to get help to get them out. Oh, Mom, Sam hit his head. Joey said there's blood."

"Run out front and blow on the horn. I told your father that would be our signal. I'll call the emergency services."

"Mom, what'll I do if Sam's dead."

"It'd take more than that to take Sam out." Margaret said, hurrying to the phone.

Lisa headed for the front, hoping her mother was right.

"Tell them to hurry," she said.

She leaned on the horn for a long moment, then pounded it in short bursts. Neighbors came running from all direction. As soon as the first one was close, she explained.

In less than five minutes, three men and two coils of rope were heading across the field. Lisa had only stopped to put on a pair of her mother's shoes at her mother's insistence before leading the way.

She wanted to run, but one of the neighbors was too old for that. Settling for a quick pace she hurried back to the two she loved most in the world.

When she reached the stable area near the cave in, she held

her breath as she looked over. Joey sat beside Sam, and the water had risen until it almost touched Sam's boots.

"We're back," she called.

Al Thompson quickly organized things. He himself went over the edge, tied firmly with one of the rope and eased over by the three men who remained on top with Lisa. She wanted to go down, but they insisted she'd be more help on top when Joey came up.

Once Al reached the surface with Joey in his arms, Lisa burst into tears and reached for her son. Squeezing him until he complained, she tried to absorb his very essence in to her body.

"Sam?" She asked Al.

"He's still unconscious. I hope those paramedics arrive soon. The water's rising." He glanced toward the distant mountains. "Must be a humdinger of a storm. I don't think we've had water here since the last of the spring rains."

"Joey can stay up here with the others. I need to go to Sam." She said, placing her son on the ground, telling him to stay by Mr. Potter, a neighbor Joey knew.

"Now Lisa, there's nothing you can do."

"I have to get to Sam!"

She reached for the rope and tried to walk down the face of the bluff as Al had. She scraped one elbow when she banged into an outcropping. Skinned her knee against the abrasive dirt, but reached the bottom without a major mishap. She unfastened the rope and ran over to the man she loved.

"Sam?"

His hat was several yards away. His eyes were closed. She could see a small pool of blood beneath his head and the rock he'd landed on.

Hoping against hope that it wasn't as serious as it looked, she took his hand in hers, searching for a pulse. It was strong and steady.

Almost collapsing with relief, she cradled his hand against her breasts.

"Sam, can you hear me? Wake up. You're scaring me."

He remained motionless.

"Sam? I love you."

He didn't move.

"I didn't need that much time to decide. You've scared me. And made me realize how fleeting life can be. What if you died now? We'd have wasted so much time. My fault. But it's a mistake I can remedy. I love you, Sam. Wake up, Please? Wake up and ask me again!"

Thirteen

The paramedics arrived without fanfare. Working in tandem, they lowered a stretcher, fixed guide ropes and soon had Sam at the top of the bluff.

The water continued to rise, covering the bottom of the arroyo. It was cold and muddy, but Lisa didn't even notice. She went up after Sam, worried because he still hadn't regained consciousness. She fervently prayed as she scrambled to the top.

The ambulance was already crossing the field when she reached level ground. Her father and mother were waiting with their car.

"Come on, honey, the paramedics said you and Joey were to come to the emergency room as well," her father said.

She felt dazed, but not hurt. Except....

She looked down, her knee was scraped, and various bumps and bruises began to be felt. She'd never be able to wear this outfit to church again.

"How's Sam?"

"Too early to tell," her father said, ushering her into the back seat. Joey was already there, in his car seat.

"Is Daddy better?" he asked forlornly.

"He will be. We'll go to the hospital now and check on him, okay?" she said, trying to keep the anguish from her tone.

Sam had to be all right. She couldn't imagine a world

without him in it.

Her mother looked back over the seat. "How are you?"

"S-C-A-R-E-D," she spelled, looking after the ambulance.

"He'll get the best attention at the hospital," Margaret said.

"I know. But what if--"

She couldn't say the words. Couldn't even think them. And especially not in front of her son. She gripped her hands tightly together. Sam had to be all right. *He had to be!*

The ride to the hospital seemed endless, but in fact took less than ten minutes. Stopping near the emergency entrance, her father quickly parked and opened her door while her mother took care of Joey.

The emergency room was bustling. One look at her and the nurses whisked her into a cubicle, Joey and Margaret right behind them.

Quickly explaining what'd happened, Lisa insisted they check Joey over first. He was the one who had tumbled all the way down with Sam.

In no time, the doctor pronounced him fine.

Lisa burst into tears. She hugged her son and only reluctantly releasing him to let her mother take him when the doctor wanted to examine her.

"How's Sam Haller?" she asked as the nurse cleaned up the abrasions.

"Came in right before you?"

"Yes, he's Joey's father. Joey's all right because Sam sheltered him somehow on the fall. He was unconscious for a long time. Has he regained consciousness?"

"I'll get someone to check," the doctor offered, nodding at the nurse.

By the time Lisa had her scraped knee bandaged and

received a tetanus shot, the nurse returned. "Sam Haller's being admitted. He regained consciousness, but there is a slight concussion and we want to keep him over night for observations."

"Can I see him?"

"Not just yet. Once he's settled in, family can visit."

Lisa nodded. She slid off the examining table and thanked the doctor; then went in search of her mother and father.

"I need to see Sam," she said when she joined them in the waiting room.

"Come home and change. You'll scare him looking like that," her mother said firmly. "We'll bring you back."

"No. I need to see him as soon as I can. Can you take Joey home?"

"Yes. And I won't let him out of my sight!" her mother vowed.

"I'm nailing that gate shut as soon as we get home," her father said. "Honey, we're so sorry."

"It wasn't anyone's fault, except maybe Joey's!" she said, giving her son a familiar mother look.

"I'm sorry Mommy. I shouldn't have gone to the creek alone. Is Daddy mad at me?"

"You think about what happened, Joey. Next time you want to go to the creek, or anywhere else, you wait for a grownup to take you. Do you understand?" Lisa said firmly.

Joey nodded solemnly.

"Okay then." She kissed his cheek. "No, Daddy isn't mad at you. He's hurt from the fall. He'll be fine in no time."

She fervently hoped she was right.

By the time she reached the reception desk on the second floor, Nick and Jennifer were already there Nick pacing in front of the nurses' station.

"Lisa, are you all right?" Jennifer asked, her gaze on the

scrapes and bandages.

"Yes. Any word on Sam?"

Nick paused and glared at her. "No. Why are you here?"

"Nick," Jennifer said softly.

He looked at her and then away.

"He's worried about his brother," Jennifer excused. "Come sit down. We can't see him yet. What happened?"

Both listened attentively as Lisa explained.

Just as she finished, a doctor came down the hall.

"Nick." He smiled and crossed to shake hands, including the two women in his greeting.

"Jim. How's Sam?" Nick asked.

"Ornery as ever. He's going to be fine. But he was out for quite a while. Always better to err on the side of caution though try convincing him of that. He insists he's ready to go home."

Lisa felt the weight of the world lift from her. He was going to be all right. Thank God. She took a breath.

"Can we see him?"

Jim turned. "One person at a time and only for a few minutes. We've given him something to reduce swelling and ease the pain. His head's pounding, naturally. Took five stitches to close the gash. But barring complications, he'll be right as rain."

"When can he go home?" Nick asked.

"Tomorrow if everything checks out normal by morning. He does have a slight concussion. We want to monitor it tonight. Want to see him?"

Nick nodded.

Lisa started to protest, then closed her mouth. Nick had a right to see his brother first.

She regretted not arguing the point five minutes later when Nick returned and told Jennifer she could go in for a couple of minutes. He looked at Lisa when Jennifer left.

"Sam doesn't want to see you."

She felt as if he'd hit her. "What? Why not?"

"He asked after Joey first thing. I told him the kid was fine and that you were here. He said he didn't want to see you. That you both had said all you had to say."

"I want to see him."

Nick's expression soften fractionally. "He's going to be fine, Lisa. He looked okay to me, except for the bandage around his head. He's a bit pale, but otherwise he looks okay. However, his wishes do count. You can't see him."

She nodded and rose, feeling shaky and scared. She didn't want to leave, but there was nothing to stay for if Sam refused to see her.

"Tell him I was concerned. And there *is* more to talk about."

"I'll tell him."

She had forfeited all rights to see him.

She was no longer family.

Slowly walking down the hall, Lisa wished Sam hadn't said no. She really wanted to see him, make sure he was all right.

Tell him she loved him.

Lisa learned from Jennifer on Tuesday that Sam had gone home from the hospital Monday morning. But she heard nothing from Sam.

Wednesday she called to see how he was. Nick answered and told her he was asleep. She asked him to have Sam call.

By Friday she knew he wasn't going to. Every day she'd waited, working with one ear attuned for the phone, the hope dimming each day.

But there was Joey to consider, she thought. Was Sam planning to have him come to the ranch this next week or not?

How was he? Jennifer said when she'd told Lisa that Sam went home that he was doing all right.

He had told her to think about their relationship. She had and more quickly than he probably imagined.

She waited until after dinner Friday evening to call him. She didn't want him to be outside. Or around the men on the ranch. She knew he ate in the bunkhouse, so gave him plenty of time to return to the house before she called.

Joey was in bed so there'd be no interruptions.

The phone rang a long time. She was about to give up when it was answered.

"Hello?"

She'd met her only once, but Lisa recognized Margot's voice instantly.

"I was calling for Sam," she said.

"He's busy right now. Can I give him a message."

"This is Lisa Haller. Would you ask if he wants Joey this week?"

"I'm sure he does, he's crazy about that kid," Margot's tone was wry.

"Is he feeling all right?" Lisa hated having to ask Margot, didn't like talking with the woman. All she could see was Margot and Sam in bed. And that she'd driven him there.

But she had to know about Joey.

"Yes, he's almost back to normal. Still has a headache, but it's getting better. You know men, so macho. He was off the pain pills by Wednesday."

"Oh?"

Margot drew in her breath. "Oops. You probably didn't want to know I was staying here, did you? Someone needed to watch him. Nick had to go somewhere on business and Jennifer's still teaching, so I was drafted. It's the least I can do, according to Nick. I'm not his favorite person."

Lisa was surprised, she thought she had that honor.

"I'll tell Sam you called. He'll probably send someone into town to get Joey since he's still not driving."

Lisa hung up feeling hurt anew.

Sam needed help and hadn't called her.

Had he changed his mind about wanting to marry her?

Nick had asked Margot to come help out. Sam had obviously not rejected *her*. She'd been there all week. A week of Margot's taking care of Sam, cooking for him. Maybe a week in which they came to view things differently.

Her first instinct was to pack up and move away from Tumbleweed again.

She shook her head. Hadn't she learned anything? If Sam didn't want her, then so be it. She'd learn to live with that.

But Joey deserved to know his father, to grow up on the ranch that'd one day be partially his. To know his uncle Nick and his grandparents.

She'd stay, continue to work for Bill and make a home for her son.

If it was hard, she'd learn to do hard things.

Lisa was lonelier than ever the next week. Joey had gone off with Jose Saturday morning. He'd called on Tuesday night and again Friday. But neither time had Sam asked to talk to her.

She listened with mingled emotions as Joey joyfully related how he helped his father and where they'd gone. No mention of the creek. She could see the two of them together in her mind, and longed to be a part of that fantasy.

Jennifer asked if Joey could accompany them to another horse show and Lisa agreed. But when Saturday dawned she regretted it. She missed her son. Wished he'd be home soon.

When her mother called, Lisa jumped at the chance to have lunch with them.

"We don't get to do this nearly often enough, now that you're back in Tumbleweed," her mother said as she placed the chicken salad and rolls on the table on the patio. Shaded from the hot sun, the table was placed to give a view of the garden. Looking over her shoulder, Lisa noticed the gate had been boarded over.

Her mother caught her look.

"Your father did that immediately after we got home from the hospital that day. I was so worried about all of you. If anything had happened..."

"Don't worry, Mom, everything's fine."

Her mother sat at the table and took one of Lisa's hands. "Is it, honey? Is everything fine?"

Lisa opened her mouth to reassure her mother, then abruptly closed it and shook her head.

"No, everything's horribly wrong. And it's my fault and I don't know how to make it different." She eyed her mother speculatively for a moment. "Do you know Margot Pendarvis?"

Margaret nodded, her gaze steady.

Lisa took a deep breath. "She's pregnant with Sam's baby."

Margaret nodded. "It was a nine-day wonder last Christmas when it came out."

"You never told me."

Margaret shrugged, releasing her hand and reaching for a serving spoon. She heaped salad on Lisa's plate and nudged the basket of rolls closer.

"I wasn't sure you wanted to hear that. At first I thought Sam had moved on. But then it looked like Margot didn't want marriage. The boy looked so unhappy for a long time."

"The boy is thirty-two years old--old enough to know better," Lisa said with asperity.

191

"Maybe, but mistakes happen. What did you want him to do, Lisa, remain a monk the rest of his life?"

"What I really want is for him to marry me again."

Margaret looked amazed. "You're kidding."

Lisa shook her head, glad to have it out in the open.

"I should never have left in the first place."

"You were very sure of yourself two years ago."

"I know. I thought I was. But two years on my own taught me a lot, Mom. A lot about life and a lot about myself. I was too immature when we got married. You and Dad told me that, but I wouldn't listen. But I've grown up and understand a lot of things I didn't before."

"Sam doesn't come unencumbered this time around," Margaret said gently.

"I know. That's a stumbling block, but only that. I'll have to deal with it if I want him."

She picked up her fork and leaned forward a bit. "And I do want him in every way and forever."

"Well, then." Margaret began to eat as if she couldn't think of anything else to say.

"Only, I'm not sure he still wants me," Lisa said a moment later.

"One way to find out go ask him," her mother suggested.

"I've been thinking about it. I sort of wanted some sign from him that he's still interested. Before we came home that Sunday, he said he was still interested. But he didn't want to see me at the hospital, so I don't know what to think. And since then, he's not called, or even answered the phone when I call the ranch."

"You have to be careful with people's hearts, Lisa. I suspect you hurt Sam more than you know when you left. He's not an easy man to know. He's not open and trusting like Nick. Remember some of the things Nick would say when he'd hang around you in high school? Sam had a difficult row to hoe with their father."

"It would serve me right if he doesn't want anything to do with me again. But I've got to find out."

"So eat up and head for the ranch."

"They're all at Jennifer's horse show. I'd like to go see her perform sometime."

"I understand she's quite good and quite crazy about horses."

"And Nick."

Margaret nodded. "The wedding's in just a couple of weeks. Nick sent an invitation to your father and me."

"Not me."

"Do you want to go?"

"Not unless things are settled between Sam and me. I'm not Nick's favorite person these days. Blood's thicker than friendship."

"As it should be," her mother said. "But love is the strongest bond of them all. If you love Sam, you need to do your best to make sure he knows that."

"I plan to do just that, Mom!"

Sunday morning, Sam fixed Joey pancakes. He wasn't much of a cook, preferring to eat in the mess hall with the men, but he liked spending time alone with his son. And Joey loved pancakes.

"Make them look like a cat, Daddy," Joey said.

He stood on a stool near the stove, critically watching Sam's every move. If Sam deviated from the established routine, Joey was quick to point it out.

"One cat coming up. Did I tell you about the cat I caught up on the ridge?"

Joey grinned and nodded. "A giant cat ready to spring and kill all the cattle. And you caught it!"

"That's right," Sam said gravely, launching into the tale once again. His son loved to hear stories about the ranch. He was glad he was here to hear them.

Sam still hadn't gotten over the fear that had swept through him when the edge of the arroyo had given way. Fear for his son's life.

"After breakfast, we'll get you dressed and head for town. I bet your mom misses you," Sam said a little later as they were eating.

"Naw, she works all the time."

"But she makes time for you."

Joey shrugged and swished a bite around in the syrup. "I like it here better. Can't I stay?"

"We're taking turns, remember? You stay with your mom and then with me."

"That's dumb."

"Don't I know it," Sam murmured beneath his breath.

He hadn't seen or spoken to Lisa in two weeks. He wondered how he was going to go the rest of his life without her especially if she stayed in Tumbleweed. Which it looked like she planned to do.

He'd tried, but she had been adamant in refusing to even consider giving them a chance since learning about the new baby. He sighed and stared at his son. His wife should be sharing breakfast with them. She should be laughing at Joey's comments and admonishing him to sit up straight.

And she should look up at him and smile--the two of them sharing the moment.

Sam put down his fork. He was going into town. He was going to talk to Lisa until he was blue in the face. One way or another, he was going to convince her to give them another chance.

She had a right to be angry about Margot. But she also had to get over it and move on. With him!

"Come on, Joey, let's get you dressed.

Lisa buttoned the shirt and studied it in the mirror. It was the fourth one she'd tried on. She wanted to look just right--not too obvious, not too casual. This one would have to do.

She brushed her hair, double checked her makeup and took a deep breath. She was as ready as she would ever be.

Heading out of town, she swung into a convenience store and bought a new toy for Joey to keep him occupied while she talked with his father.

On the road again, she felt anticipation rise. She was going to flat-out ask Sam if he still wanted to marry her. There were lot of things they needed to discuss, and decision to make, but being apart was not an option she wanted to explore. Been there, done that. Didn't like it at all.

She loved Sam Haller, stumbling block and all. It'd be up to her to make the first step and she was ready today.

The ranch was quiet when she arrived. She passed Nick's place, noticing Jennifer's car parked on the side. In another two weeks, school would be out and they'd be married and setting up house together.

If she hadn't been so focused on her quest, she'd have spared a moment to envy them starting out fresh, deeply in love, with their whole lives ahead of them.

Not so with her and Sam. They had a past. One that wouldn't ever go away.

But one from which they could learn and grow and move on.

And if he didn't love her, she had enough love for the both of them. She felt almost giddy with excitement.

Stopping by the house, she killed the engine, looking for Sam's truck. It wasn't parked in its usual place.

Slowly she climbed out of her car and headed for the front door. She rang the bell and waited. The echoing silence was her only response.

Trying again, she waited impatiently. Where were they? Had he taken Joey on a ride before heading to town?

Slowly wandering to the barn, she saw two cowboys working on one of the stalls.

"Hi. Have you seen Sam?"

"Not today," one replied. The other shook his head. "Try the house," he offered.

"I did, there's no answer. Did he take a horse to ride somewhere?"

One man shrugged. "Check the corral. There should be seventeen horses. If one is missing, maybe he did."

"He usually takes that big black."

Lisa nodded. She knew Sam's favorite horse.

Checking the horses in the corral, she saw his horse. But upon counting, there were only sixteen horses. Had he taken another one this morning?

She went back to the porch and sat on the top step. She'd come this far. She wasn't going to be turned back until she'd talked to him.

"I need to go potty, Daddy," Joey said plaintively.

"Your mother isn't home and neither is Jennifer. Do you know anyone else in the house that would let you in?" Sam asked.

They'd been waiting more than an hour for Lisa. He'd

called her mother's place earlier, but Margaret hadn't seen Lisa, nor spoken with her that morning.

He drove around town once, checking at the grocery store. Her car wasn't there either.

Where was she?

He leaned against the porch railing and looked down the street once more. "We can go to the cafe in town and get something to eat. And you can go potty," he told Joey.

"Okay. I want a hamburger."

Forty minutes later they were back. Still no sign of Lisa's car. Sam sat on the top step and watched Joey play in the year. It wasn't a ranch, but it at least afforded him room to run and play. Better than the apartment he'd seen in Fort Worth.

Where was Lisa?

Had she gone out with someone else?

The thought made him feel sick. He'd tried to talk to her before the accident. She'd made no effort since to contact him.

How clear did a man need it to be?

A lot clearer, he thought. He wanted to see her, touch her, kiss her. Then ask her again. Or maybe he shouldn't ask again, just move in with her until she agreed to move out to the ranch with him.

"No, it's marriage or nothing," he said.

"What, Daddy?" Joey asked, pausing in his game.

"Nothing, just wondering where your mother is."

"If she doesn't come home, can I go back to the ranch with you?"

"Sure, partner."

If she doesn't come home, he wanted to know why no one had mentioned Lisa dating anyone. She'd said she hadn't dated during their two years apart.

Not like him who had tried to drive her memory away by making as many new ones as he could.

He was determined he was going to see her today. Even if they waited until dark!

As the hours ticked slowly by, Lisa grew uncertain. Maybe this had been a bad idea. Obviously Sam wasn't around. Had he called her after she'd left that morning to tell her where he and Joey were going? She checked her phone—it was dead. Blast it. Now what?

Finally around two, she gave up and headed back to town.

Turning on her street, the first thing she noticed was Joey running in the yard. Then Sam's truck. Then Sam sitting on the top step of her apartment house.

Instantly anticipation rose. She licked her lips, knowing she'd worn off all traces of lipstick. Darn the man, what was he doing here?

The carefully rehearsed words fled. Heart pounding, she stopped the car and climbed out, her eyes meeting Sam's holding them as she walked around the front of the car and started toward the porch.

"Where have you been?" he roared, coming up in one swift movement.

Fourteen

"Where have *I* been?" she asked, stopping and putting her fists on her hips. "I like that. How long have you been here?"

"It seems like forever. Out with a date?"

Lisa almost burst out laughing. "That's a joke, right? I've been sitting on your front porch since nine o'clock this morning!"

He looked at her.

"Hi, Mommy,"

Joey ran over to give her a hug, then ran back to his game.

One side of Sam's mouth lifted in a half smile. Her heart skidded began beating frantically. He was a beautiful man.

"We've been here since about then. We must have passed each other."

She blinked. Some of her indignation faded.

"You've been here? Why?"

He walked down the steps and met her on the walkway. "Why were you at the ranch?"

"I wanted to talk to you."

"About time."

"What?"

"I said about time. I've been waiting for two weeks for you to want to talk to me," he said.

She frowned. "I don't think so, buster. I wanted to talk to you at the hospital. I called during the week. Left messages."

He reached out and brushed a strand of hair off her check, his fingertips gentle against her skin. "I didn't know that."

"Nick said you didn't want to see me," she said, memorized by the flame in his eyes.

"Oh, I wanted to see you, Lisa. I wanted to more than see you."

He pulled her into his arms and kissed her.

Lisa threw her arms around him and held on tight. She kissed him with all the pent up love and heartache and uncertainty in her.

This is where she belonged. This is where she longed to be--right with Sam forever.

Sanity returned slowly. He leaned back and gazed into her eyes.

"I need to talk to you," he said.

"Yes."

"I want you to marry me again. I'm crazy about you. And you still feel something for me, I know it."

"Yes."

"And this bit about Joey spending one week at the ranch and one week here is for the birds. He needs both parents and we owe it to him to provide him a safe, secure home."

"I agree."

"So no arguments, I want you to marry me and stay with me forever this time."

"Yes."

He pulled back and tilted his head to one side. "Are you all right?"

"Yes." She laughed joyfully. "Yes, to getting married. Yes, to giving Joey a united family. Yes, to living on the ranch, and yes to being crazy about you. That's why I went to the ranch. I was going to talk to you about that very thing. I love you, Sam. I did before, I did while we were apart and I still do. That obviously isn't going to change no matter what."

"I'm crazy about you, Lisa Haller." He kissed her quickly, then picked her up and spun her around.

Her shrieks of laughter drew Joey's attention.

"Daddy, swing me, too!" he yelled, running over to his parents.

"Sure thing, partner. Guess what? Your mama just agreed to come to the ranch. We're all going to live there, what do you think about that?"

Sam picked his son up and held the two of them in his arms.

"Really?" Joey's eyes grew big as he looked from Sam to Lisa.

"Really," she concurred. "As soon as your daddy and I get married."

"Not today, huh?" Sam asked, his eyes twinkling.

"Not today. But soon?"

"Soon as we can make it. I'll call about getting a license first thing tomorrow. Wish the courthouse was open today."

Lisa felt sheltered in the arms of the man she loved. True, he hadn't said he loved her. But maybe he didn't know the words. Or the feelings.

"Sam?"

"Yes?"

"Do you like me more than your horse?"

He looked at her as if she'd gone crazy.

"What kind of dumb fool question is that? Of course I like you better than my horse."

"Better than Nick?"

He took a moment to consider the question, his eyes narrowing. "Maybe. Different, that's for sure."

Lisa smiled. "How about Joey?"

"Same different, but yeah, maybe a shade better. What's got into you?"

"Nothing."

He loved her. He just didn't say the words. 'Crazy about you' would have to do.

Her love blossomed and consumed her as she reached up to kiss him gently on the lips. "I'm crazy about you, cowboy," she whispered.

"Me, too, babe. Me, too!" He hesitated a minute, then set Joey down. "Run play, Joey. I have something else to talk about with your mom."

"When can we go to the ranch?"

"Later. We'll go back later."

Lisa watched as Joey ran across the yard, yelling his delight. How could she have taken her son from his father? She'd never leave again.

"Lisa, there's still the new baby," Sam said.

"I know. I've thought about it a lot. You're right, I'll probably fall in love with it the moment it's born."

"I'd change that if I could."

She nodded. "I know you would. But we can't. And the situation's of our own making. Each has a responsibility to it. But I love you more than I'm jealous of Margot."

"You needn't be jealous, sweetheart. I tried to replace you, but couldn't. Margot's just a wild girl who got caught."

"Is two kids all you want?"

"I want a house full, how about you?"

Lisa nodded. Things would work out. She'd make sure this time.

Epilogue

Two Years Later....

"Mommy, Mommy, Daddy's coming!" Little Holly Haller jumped up and down on the porch in her excitement as she spotted Sam heading for the house from the barn. Joey ran along side him, talking nineteen to the dozen as usual.

Lisa stayed on the rocker, keeping an eye on Holly so she didn't get too excited and tumble off the steps. She'd done that once months ago when first learning to walk and scared six months out of Lisa.

"He'll be here in a minute, honey, don't get near the edge."

Holly spun around and ran to Lisa, flinging her arms up.

"Up!" she demanded.

Despite her bulk, Lisa readily complied. She loved holding this child of her heart. Holly was sweet and loving and a joy to be around. The prophesy had come true. Lisa had fallen in love with Holly the day she was born--the very moment, she often thought. Margot had graciously allowed both Sam and Lisa to be in the delivery room. She'd signed the adoption papers while still in the hospital.

Every once in a while she'd drop by to see her daughter, but she had no regrets about relinquishing her care to Lisa and Sam.

"So how are my girls today?" Sam asked, stepping up on the porch.

"I painted, Daddy," Holly said, struggling to get down as quickly as she had to get up.

Lisa laughed and reached up her hands. These days she needed assistance in getting up.

"We had a lovely day, thank you. How about you and Joey?"

"He rode all the way to the property line without a lead, right partner?" Sam asked.

"I did, Mommy. I can ride all by myself now."

At five, he was growing so fast she could hardly believe it. In September, he'd start school. She'd miss him being around all the time, but by then, his new brother or sister would have arrived to fill up her time. With Holly just two and a new baby, she'd have plenty to do.

And Sam. She spent as much time as she could with Sam. They had so much they liked doing together, she almost resented the time they spent apart.

But the ranch and her work did place certain demands.

Which made their time together to be all the sweeter, she'd decided long ago.

Sam kissed her, rubbing her swollen belly gently. "I'm crazy about you," he said for her ears alone.

If you liked **Crazy About a Cowboy**,
you'll love the next book in the *Cowboy Hero* series,
Never Doubt a Cowboy.

If you enjoyed **Crazy About a Cowboy** please consider leaving a review.

More Books by Barbara McMahon

Cowboy Hero Series
The Cowboy Next Door
Cowboy's Bride
One Stubborn Cowboy
Crazy About a Cowboy
Never Doubt a Cowboy
Cowboy Marshal
Summer Cowboy
Second Chance Cowboy
Movie Star Cowboy

Cowboys of Wildcat Creek
Valentine's Cowboy Rescue
Shelly and the Cowboy
Kristi's Cowboy Hero
Holly's Reluctant Cowboy
A Cowboy for Eliza

Sweet Reunion Romance Collection
Unexpected Reunion
Unpredictable Reunion
Unanticipated Reunion

The Harts of Texas Series
Rebel Heart
Tangled Hearts
Reckless Heart

Ultimate Billionaires Series
The Cynical Sheikh
Falling for the Sheikh
A Sheikh of Her Own
The Unforgettable Sheikh

Rocky Point Series
Rocky Point Legacy
Rocky Point Reunion
Rocky Point Promise
Rocky Point Hero
Rocky Point Inn
Rocky Point Dawn

The Talmadge Sisters Series
Letters to Caroline
Michelle's Marriage Deal
Trusting Abby

Tropical Escapes Series
Island Rendezvous
Come into the Sun
Island Paradise

A Sweet Clean Christmas Romance Collection
The Christmas Cop
The Cowboy's Special Christmas
A Soldier's Christmas
A Teaspoon of Mistletoe
The Christmas Locket
A Key West Christmas

Sweet Romance Stand-alone Collection
Because of You
Cowboy Charade
I'll Take Forever
Jared's Promise
Mail Order Bride
Not Really Married
Sweet Meant To Be
The Cowboy Comes Home
The Paper Marriage
Trusting Jake
The Banished Bride